NANCY DREW

girl detective

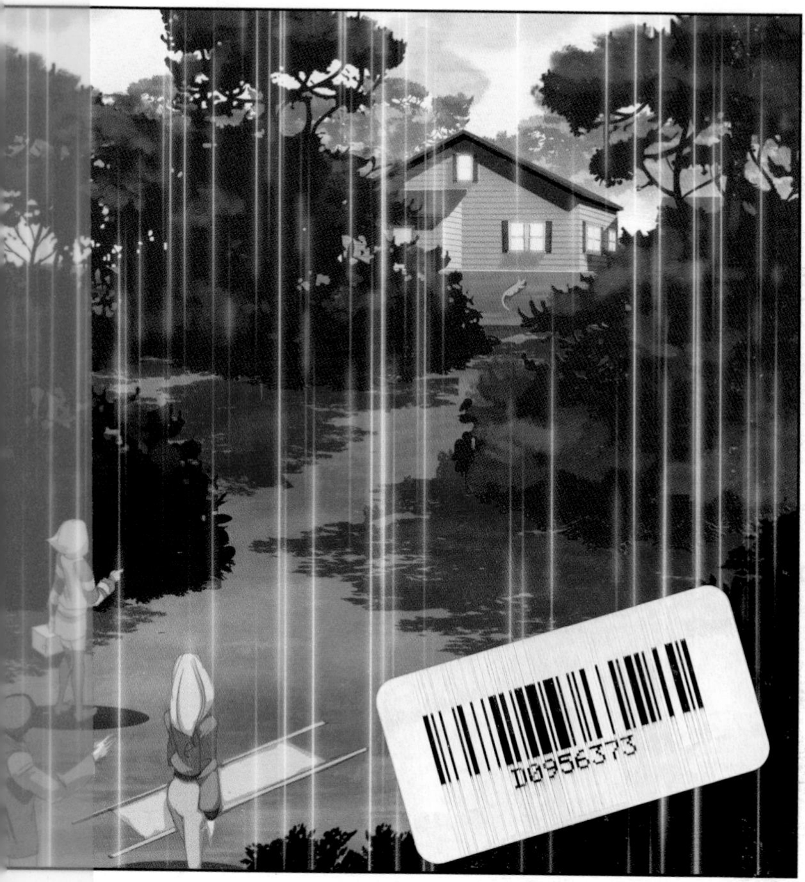

PAPERCUTZ™

NANCY DREW GRAPHIC NOVELS AVAILABLE FROM PAPERCUTZ

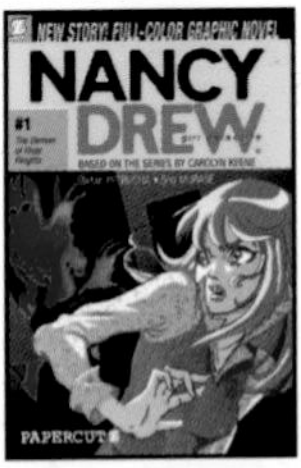
NEW STORY! FULL-COLOR GRAPHIC NOVEL
NANCY
DREW
PAPERCUTZ

#1 “The Demon of River Heights”

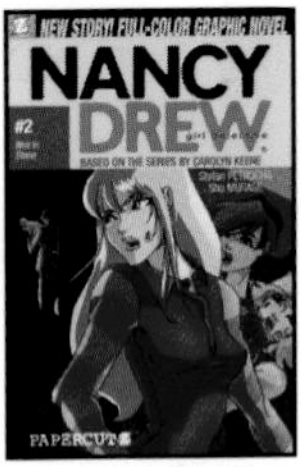
NEW STORY! FULL-COLOR GRAPHIC NOVEL
NANCY
DREW
PAPERCUTZ

#2 “Writ In Stone”

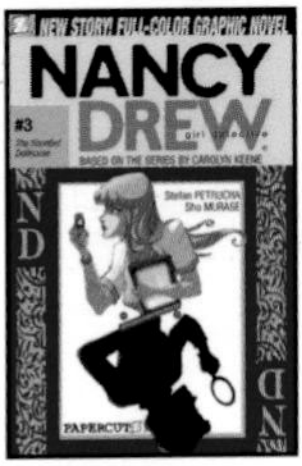
NEW STORY! FULL-COLOR GRAPHIC NOVEL
NANCY
DREW
PAPERCUTZ

#3 “The Haunted Dollhouse”

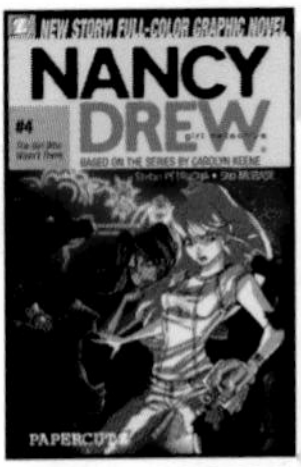
NEW STORY! FULL-COLOR GRAPHIC NOVEL
NANCY
DREW
PAPERCUTZ

#4 “The Girl Wh Wasn’t There”

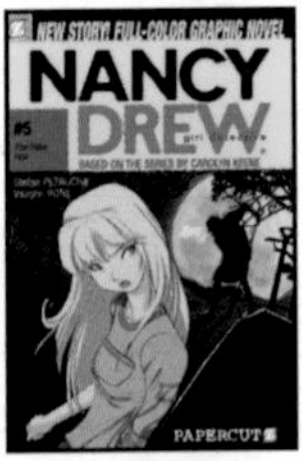
NEW STORY! FULL-COLOR GRAPHIC NOVEL
NANCY
DREW
PAPERCUTZ

#5 “The Fake Heir”

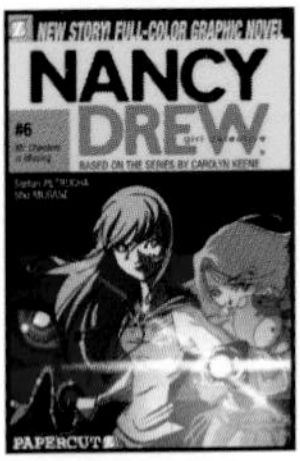
NEW STORY! FULL-COLOR GRAPHIC NOVEL
NANCY
DREW
PAPERCUTZ

#6 “Mr. Cheeters Is Missing”

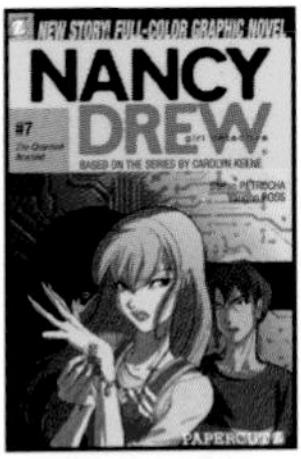
NEW STORY! FULL-COLOR GRAPHIC NOVEL
NANCY
DREW
PAPERCUTZ

#7 “The Charmed Bracelet”

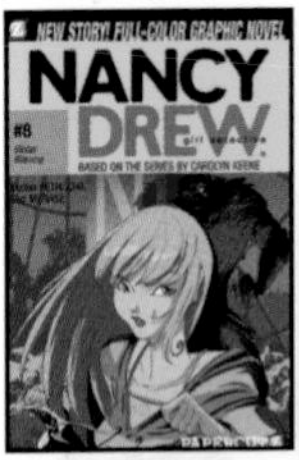
NEW STORY! FULL-COLOR GRAPHIC NOVEL
NANCY
DREW

#8 “Global Warning”

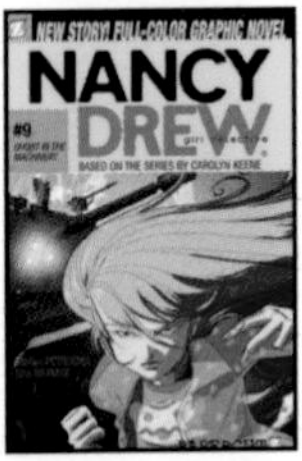
NEW STORY! FULL-COLOR GRAPHIC NOVEL
NANCY
DREW

#9 “Ghost In The Machinery”

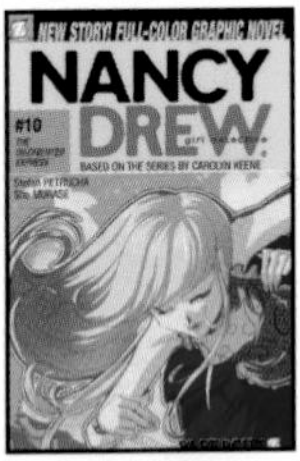
NEW STORY! FULL-COLOR GRAPHIC NOVEL
NANCY
DREW

#10 “The Disoriented Express”

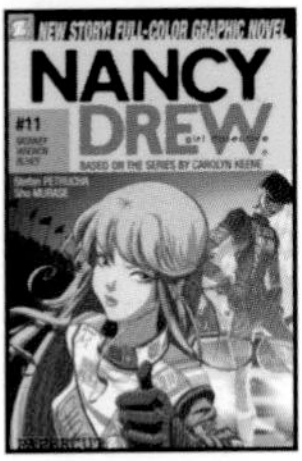
NEW STORY! FULL-COLOR GRAPHIC NOVEL
NANCY
DREW

#11 “Monkey Wrench Blues”

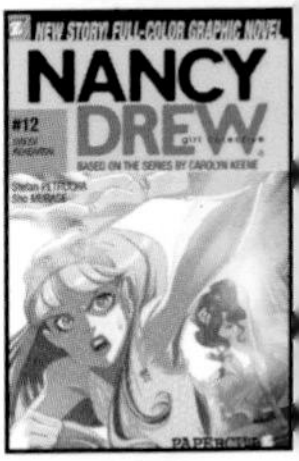
NEW STORY! FULL-COLOR GRAPHIC NOVEL
NANCY
DREW

#12 “Dress Reversal”

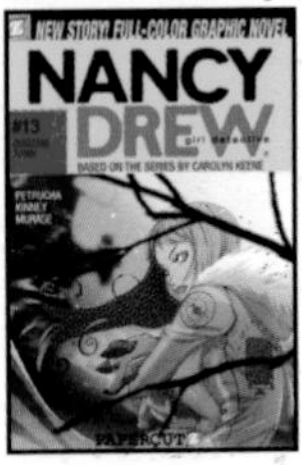
NEW STORY! FULL-COLOR GRAPHIC NOVEL
NANCY
DREW
PAPERCUTZ

#13 “Doggone Town”

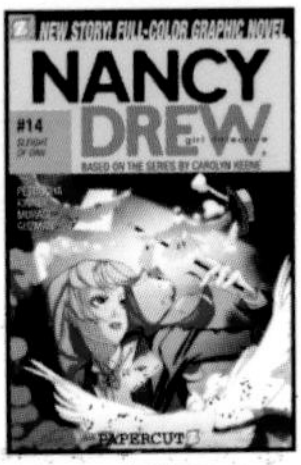
NEW STORY! FULL-COLOR GRAPHIC NOVEL
NANCY
DREW
PAPERCUTZ

#14 “Sleight of Dan”

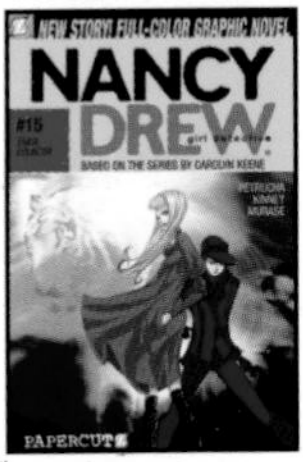
NEW STORY! FULL-COLOR GRAPHIC NOVEL
NANCY
DREW
PAPERCUTZ

#15 “Tiger Counter”

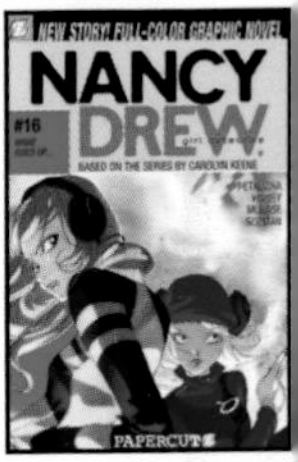
NEW STORY! FULL-COLOR GRAPHIC NOVEL
NANCY
DREW
PAPERCUTZ

Coming February
#16 “What Goes U

$7.95 each in paperback, $12.95 each in hardcover.

Please add $4.00 for postage and handling for the first book, add $1.00 for each additional bo

Please make check payable to NBM Publishing. Send to:

Papercutz, 40 Exchange Place, Suite 1308 New York, NY 10005, 1-800-886-1223

www.papercutz.com

NANCY
DREW

#15   girl detective ®

Tiger Counter

STEFAN PETRUCHA & SARAH KINNEY • Writers
SHO MURASE • Artist
with 3D CG elements and color by CARLOS JOSE GUZMAN
Based on the series by
CAROLYN KEENE

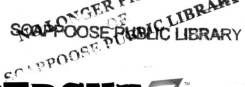

PAPERCUTZ™
New York

Tiger Counter
STEFAN PETRUCHA & SARAH KINNEY – Writers
SHO MURASE – Artist
with 3D CG elements and color by CARLOS JOSE GUZMAN
BRYAN SENKA – Letterer
MIKHAELA REID and MASHEKA WOOD – Production
MICHAEL PETRANEK - Editorial Assistant
JIM SALICRUP
Editor-in-Chief

ISBN 10: 1-59707-118-8 paperback edition
ISBN 13: 978-1-59707-118-5 paperback edition
ISBN 10: 1-59707-119-6 hardcover edition
ISBN 13: 978-1-59707-119-2 hardcover edition

Printed in China.
Distributed by Macmillan.

10   9   8   7   6   5   4   3   2   1

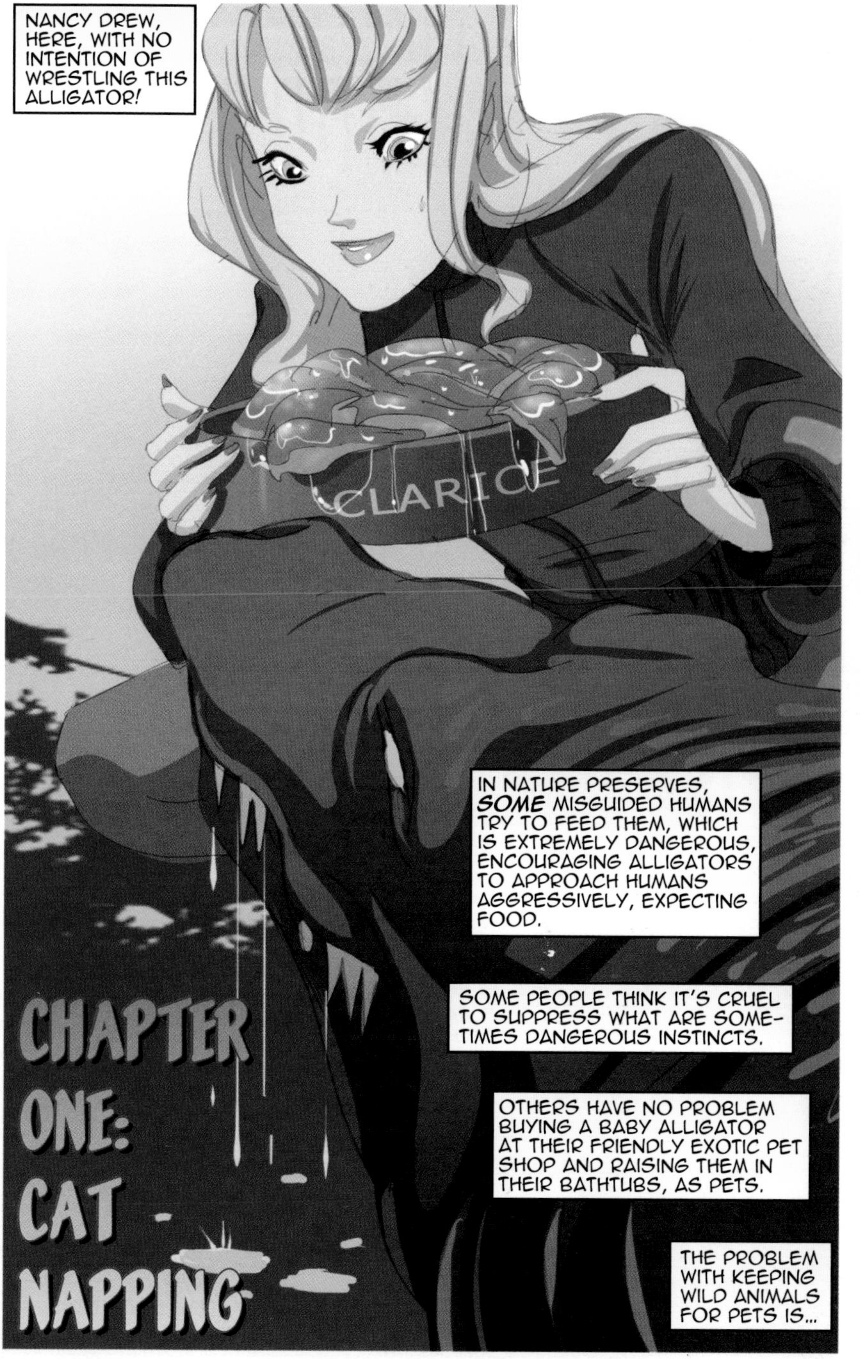
NANCY DREW, HERE, WITH NO INTENTION OF WRESTLING THIS ALLIGATOR!
CLARICE
IN NATURE PRESERVES, SOME MISGUIDED HUMANS TRY TO FEED THEM, WHICH IS EXTREMELY DANGEROUS, ENCOURAGING ALLIGATORS TO APPROACH HUMANS AGGRESSIVELY, EXPECTING FOOD.
SOME PEOPLE THINK IT'S CRUEL TO SUPPRESS WHAT ARE SOME-TIMES DANGEROUS INSTINCTS.
OTHERS HAVE NO PROBLEM BUYING A BABY ALLIGATOR AT THEIR FRIENDLY EXOTIC PET SHOP AND RAISING THEM IN THEIR BATHTUBS, AS PETS.
THE PROBLEM WITH KEEPING WILD ANIMALS FOR PETS IS...
CHAPTER ONE: CAT NAPPING

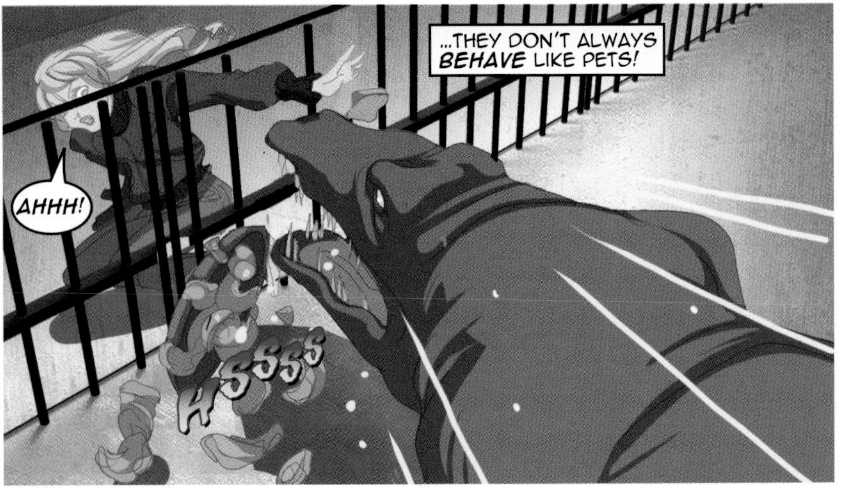
...THEY DON'T ALWAYS *BEHAVE* LIKE PETS!
AHHH!
HSSSSS

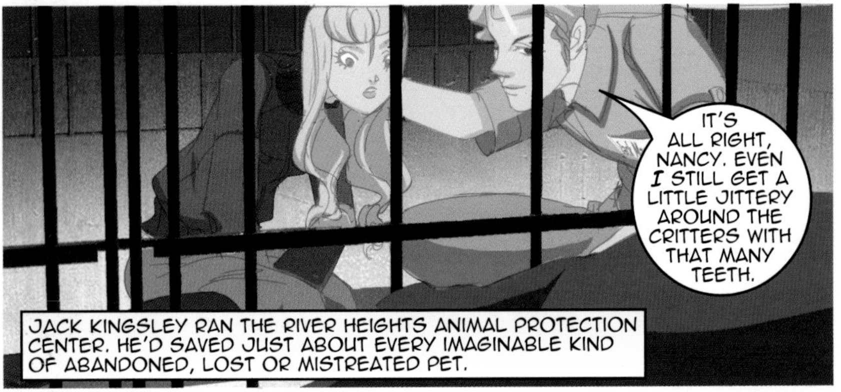
IT'S ALL RIGHT, NANCY. EVEN *I* STILL GET A LITTLE JITTERY AROUND THE CRITTERS WITH THAT MANY TEETH.
JACK KINGSLEY RAN THE RIVER HEIGHTS ANIMAL PROTECTION CENTER. HE'D SAVED JUST ABOUT EVERY IMAGINABLE KIND OF ABANDONED, LOST OR MISTREATED PET.

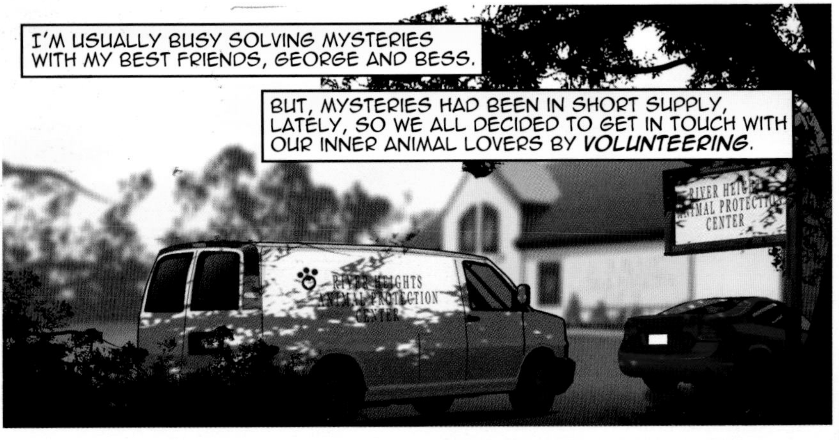
I'M USUALLY BUSY SOLVING MYSTERIES WITH MY BEST FRIENDS, GEORGE AND BESS.
BUT, MYSTERIES HAD BEEN IN SHORT SUPPLY, LATELY, SO WE ALL DECIDED TO GET IN TOUCH WITH OUR INNER ANIMAL LOVERS BY *VOLUNTEERING*.
RIVER HEIGHTS ANIMAL PROTECTION CENTER

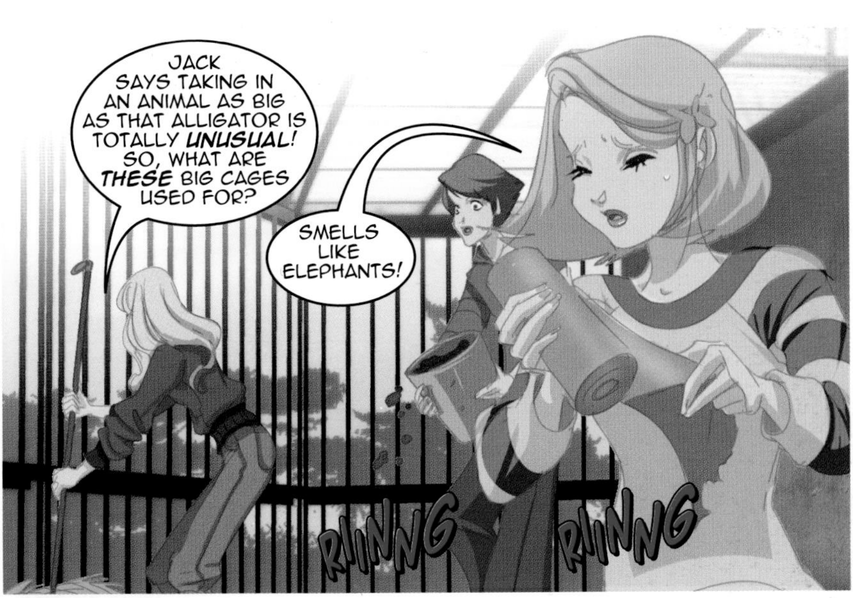
JACK SAYS TAKING IN AN ANIMAL AS BIG AS THAT ALLIGATOR IS TOTALLY *UNUSUAL*! SO, WHAT ARE *THESE* BIG CAGES USED FOR?
SMELLS LIKE ELEPHANTS!
RIINNG
RIINNG

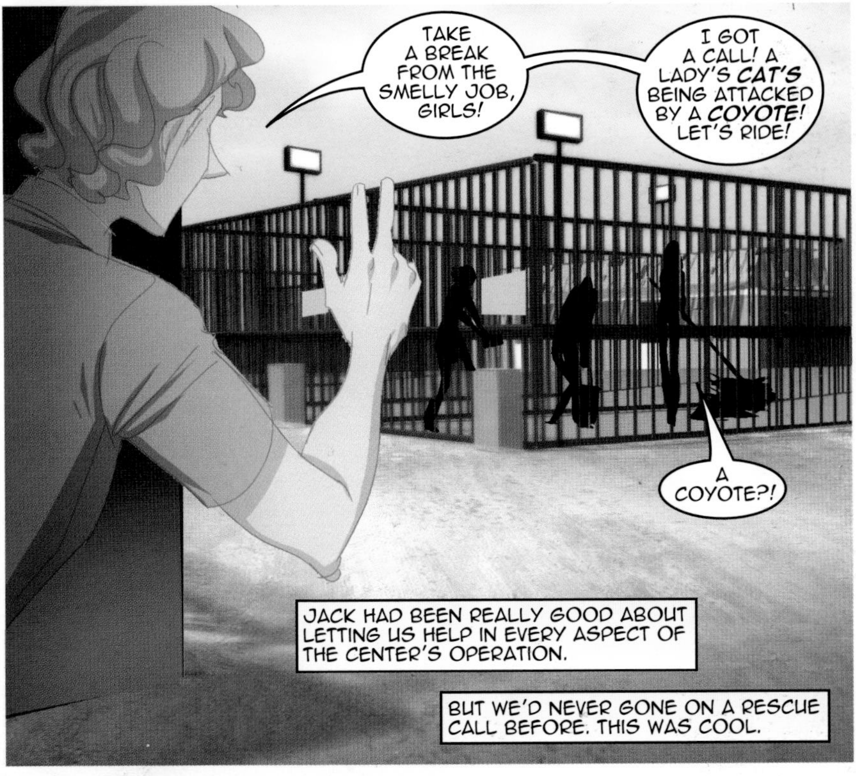
TAKE A BREAK FROM THE SMELLY JOB, GIRLS!
I GOT A CALL! A LADY'S *CAT'S* BEING ATTACKED BY A *COYOTE*! LET'S RIDE!
A COYOTE?!
JACK HAD BEEN REALLY GOOD ABOUT LETTING US HELP IN EVERY ASPECT OF THE CENTER'S OPERATION.
BUT WE'D NEVER GONE ON A RESCUE CALL BEFORE. THIS WAS COOL.

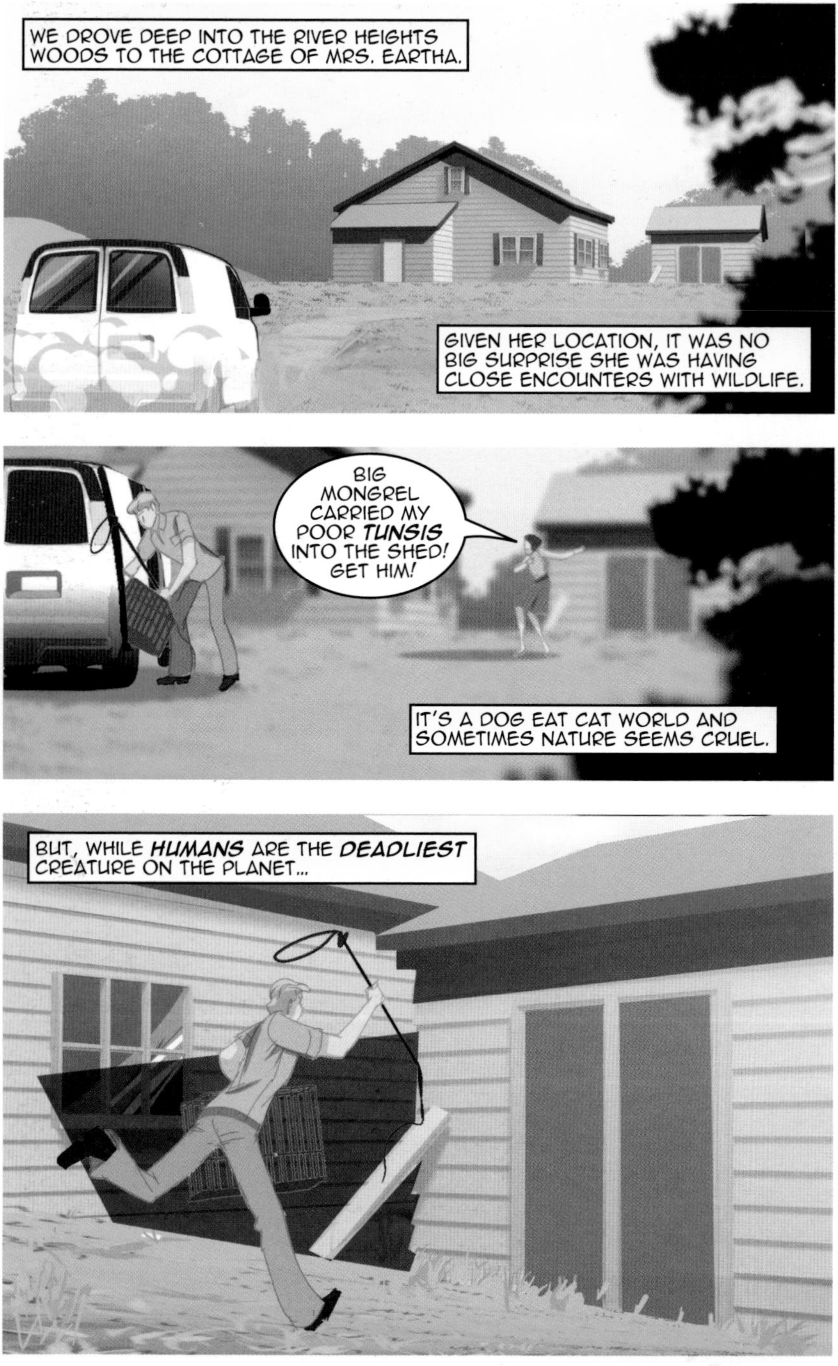
WE DROVE DEEP INTO THE RIVER HEIGHTS WOODS TO THE COTTAGE OF MRS. EARTHA.
GIVEN HER LOCATION, IT WAS NO BIG SURPRISE SHE WAS HAVING CLOSE ENCOUNTERS WITH WILDLIFE.
BIG MONGREL CARRIED MY POOR ***TUNSIS*** INTO THE SHED! GET HIM!
IT'S A DOG EAT CAT WORLD AND SOMETIMES NATURE SEEMS CRUEL.
BUT, WHILE ***HUMANS*** ARE THE ***DEADLIEST*** CREATURE ON THE PLANET...

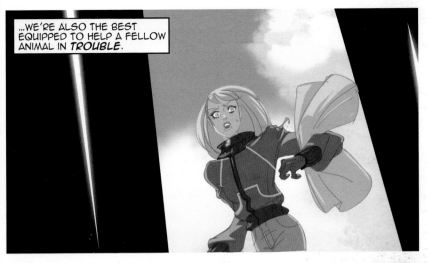

...WE'RE ALSO THE BEST EQUIPPED TO HELP A FELLOW ANIMAL IN *TROUBLE*.

HE'D CAGED THE COYOTE WITHOUT HURTING IT.

CAT'S STILL ALIVE. WRAP IT IN A TOWEL AND BRING IT IN THE HOUSE. I'LL GET THE MEDICAL KIT.

TUNSIS! CAN YOU SAVE MY TUNSIS?

WE'LL TRY.

AS A VETERINARIAN, JACK WAS ESPECIALLY GOOD AT HELPING THOSE SMALLER AND *FURRIER* THAN HIM.

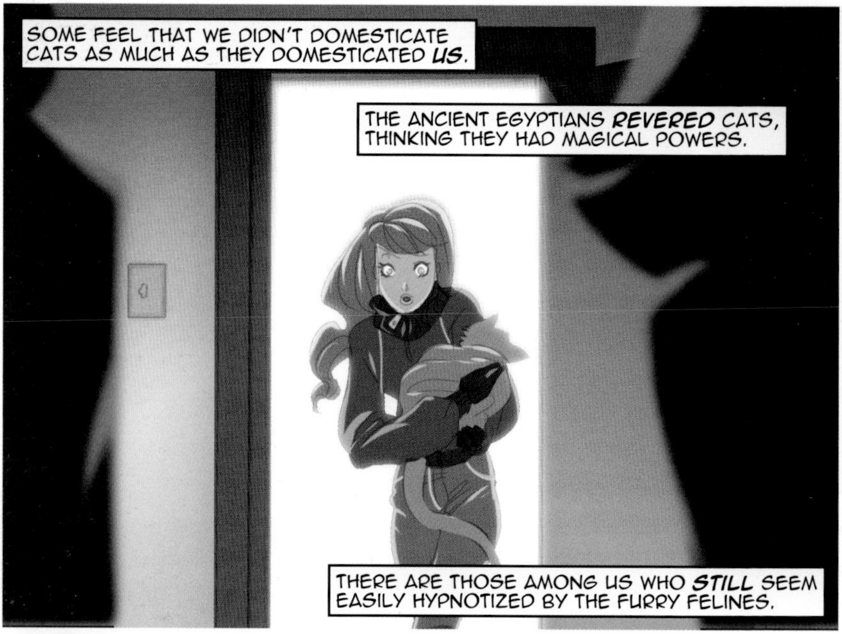
SOME FEEL THAT WE DIDN'T DOMESTICATE CATS AS MUCH AS THEY DOMESTICATED *US*.
THE ANCIENT EGYPTIANS *REVERED* CATS, THINKING THEY HAD MAGICAL POWERS.
THERE ARE THOSE AMONG US WHO *STILL* SEEM EASILY HYPNOTIZED BY THE FURRY FELINES.

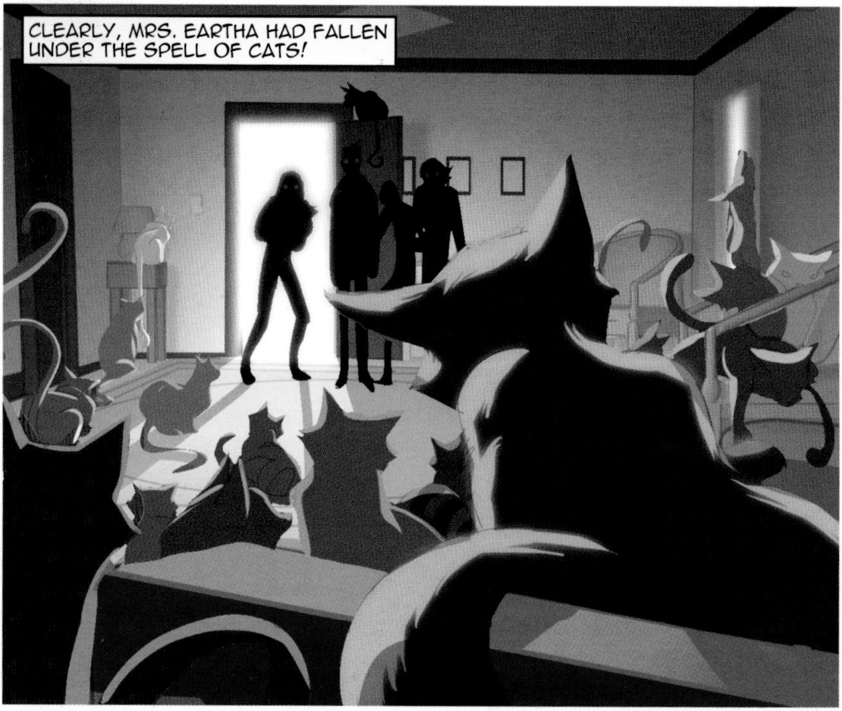
CLEARLY, MRS. EARTHA HAD FALLEN UNDER THE SPELL OF CATS!

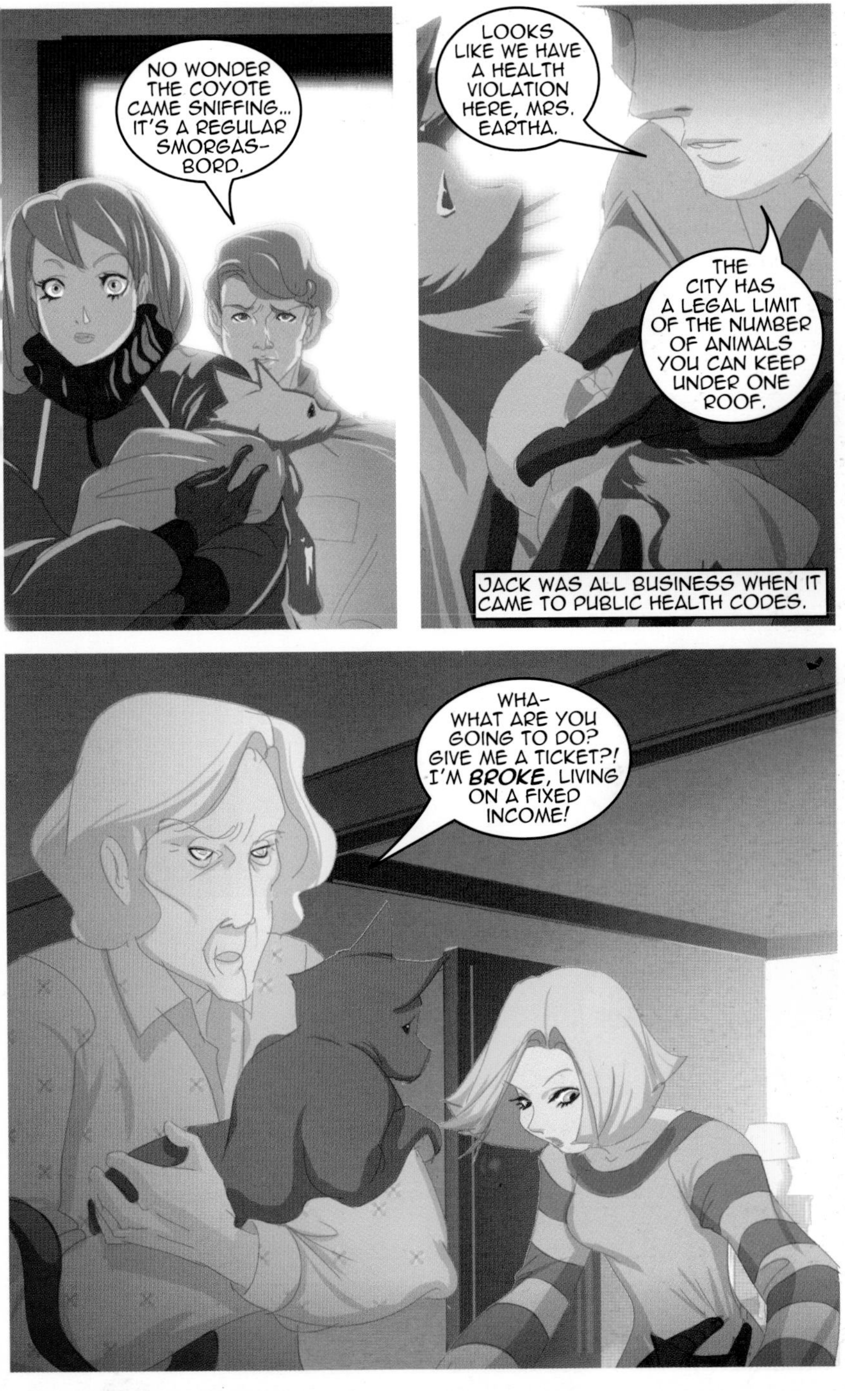
NO WONDER THE COYOTE CAME SNIFFING... IT'S A REGULAR SMORGAS-BORD.
LOOKS LIKE WE HAVE A HEALTH VIOLATION HERE, MRS. EARTHA.
THE CITY HAS A LEGAL LIMIT OF THE NUMBER OF ANIMALS YOU CAN KEEP UNDER ONE ROOF.
JACK WAS ALL BUSINESS WHEN IT CAME TO PUBLIC HEALTH CODES.
WHA- WHAT ARE YOU GOING TO DO? GIVE ME A TICKET?! I'M BROKE, LIVING ON A FIXED INCOME!

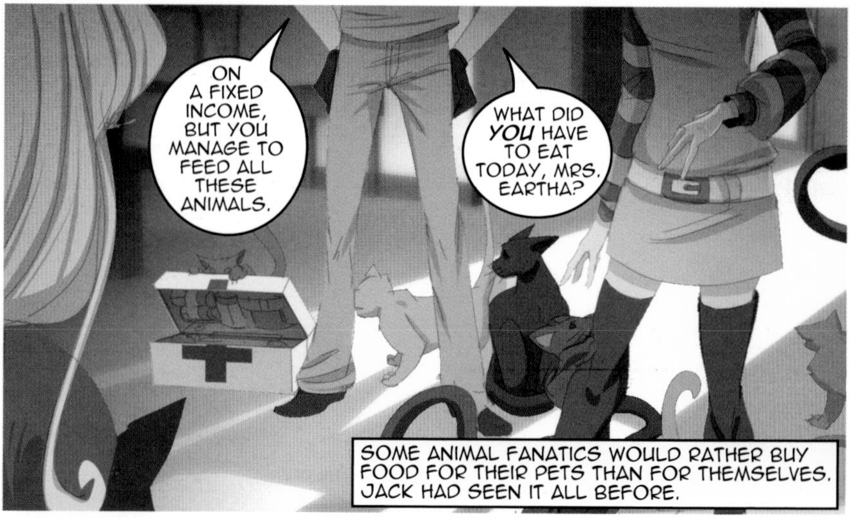
ON A FIXED INCOME, BUT YOU MANAGE TO FEED ALL THESE ANIMALS.
WHAT DID *YOU* HAVE TO EAT TODAY, MRS. EARTHA?
SOME ANIMAL FANATICS WOULD RATHER BUY FOOD FOR THEIR PETS THAN FOR THEMSELVES. JACK HAD SEEN IT ALL BEFORE.

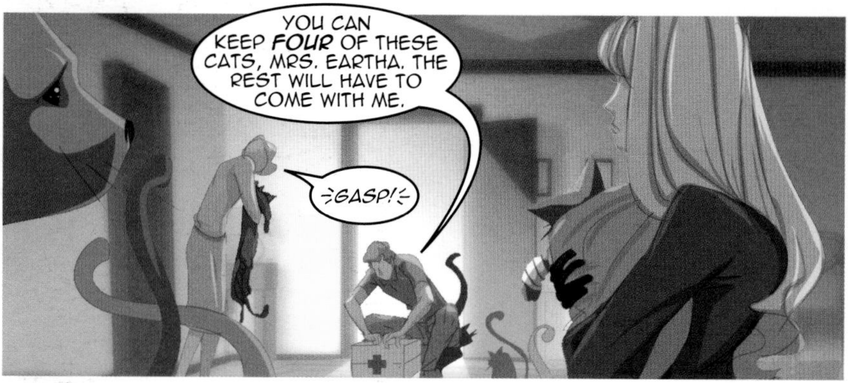
YOU CAN KEEP *FOUR* OF THESE CATS, MRS. EARTHA. THE REST WILL HAVE TO COME WITH ME.
GASP!

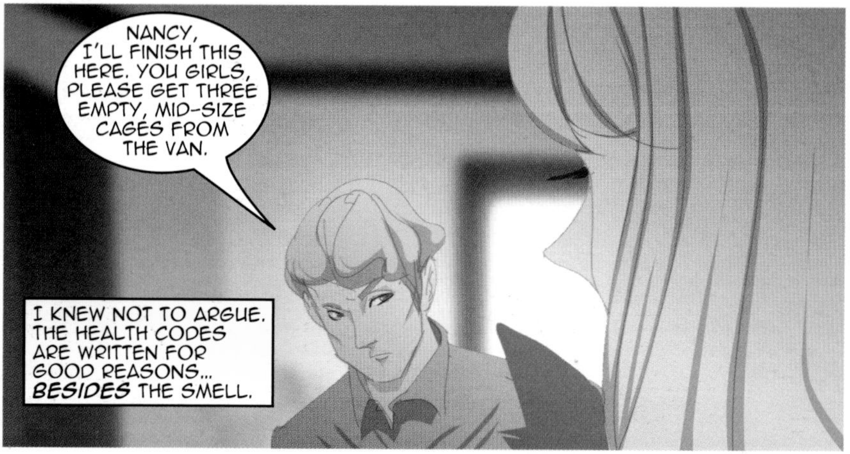
NANCY, I'LL FINISH THIS HERE. YOU GIRLS, PLEASE GET THREE EMPTY, MID-SIZE CAGES FROM THE VAN.
I KNEW NOT TO ARGUE. THE HEALTH CODES ARE WRITTEN FOR GOOD REASONS... *BESIDES* THE SMELL.

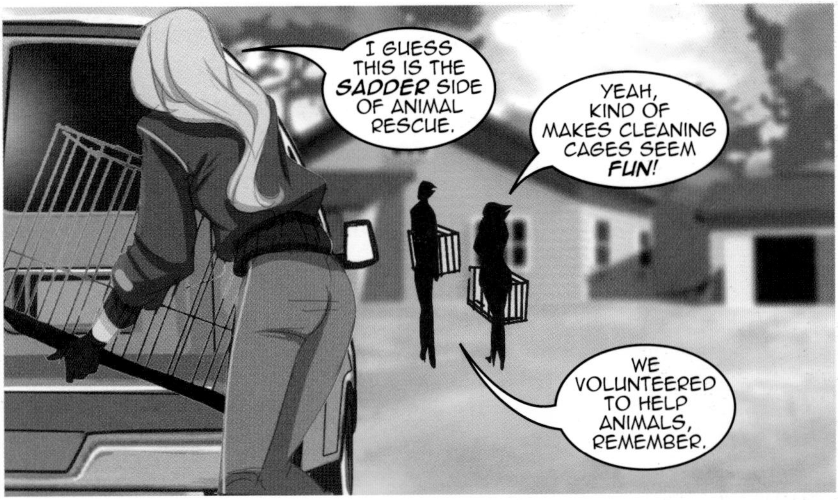
I GUESS THIS IS THE SADDER SIDE OF ANIMAL RESCUE.
YEAH, KIND OF MAKES CLEANING CAGES SEEM FUN!
WE VOLUNTEERED TO HELP ANIMALS, REMEMBER.

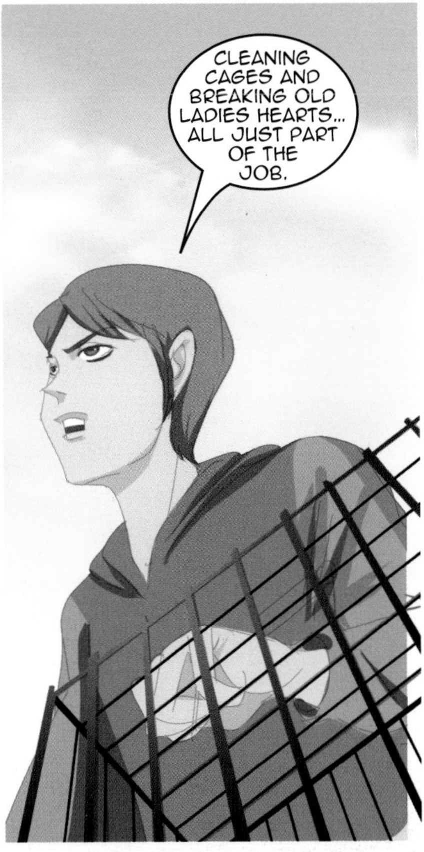
CLEANING CAGES AND BREAKING OLD LADIES HEARTS... ALL JUST PART OF THE JOB.

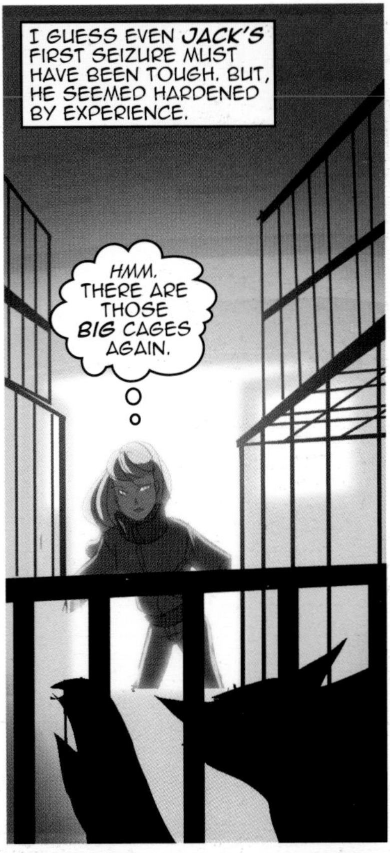
I GUESS EVEN JACK'S FIRST SEIZURE MUST HAVE BEEN TOUGH. BUT, HE SEEMED HARDENED BY EXPERIENCE.
HMM. THERE ARE THOSE BIG CAGES AGAIN.

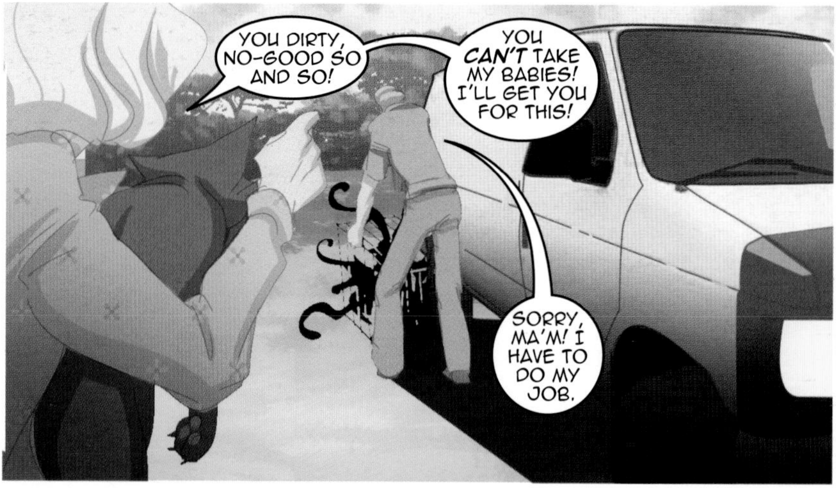
YOU DIRTY, NO-GOOD SO AND SO!
YOU CAN'T TAKE MY BABIES! I'LL GET YOU FOR THIS!
SORRY, MA'M! I HAVE TO DO MY JOB.

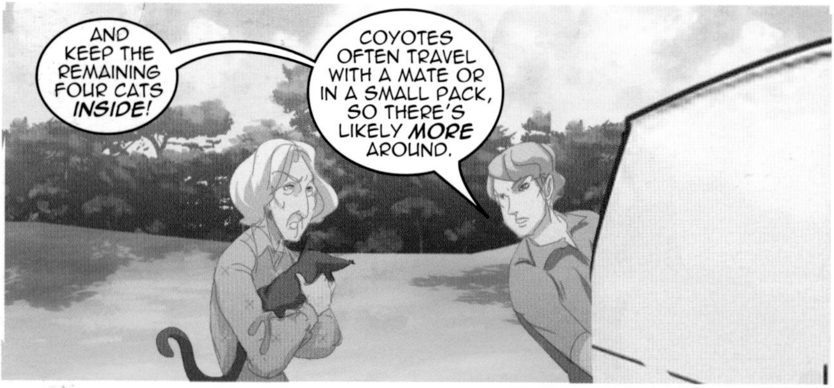
COYOTES OFTEN TRAVEL WITH A MATE OR IN A SMALL PACK, SO THERE'S LIKELY MORE AROUND.
AND KEEP THE REMAINING FOUR CATS INSIDE!

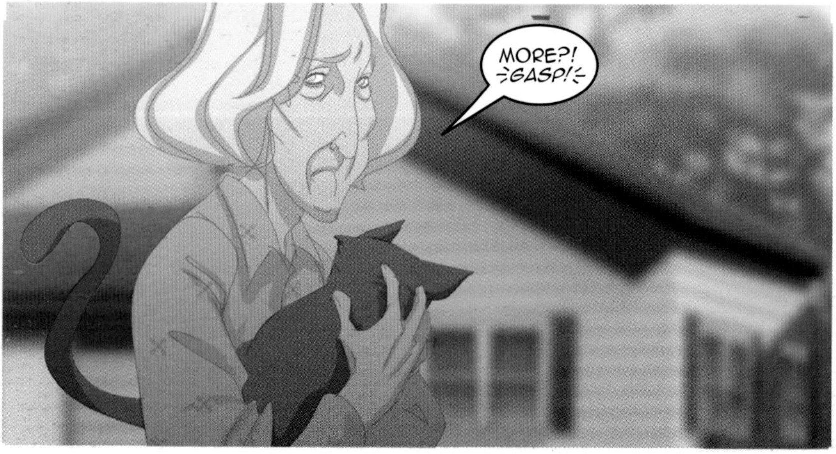
MORE?! GASP!

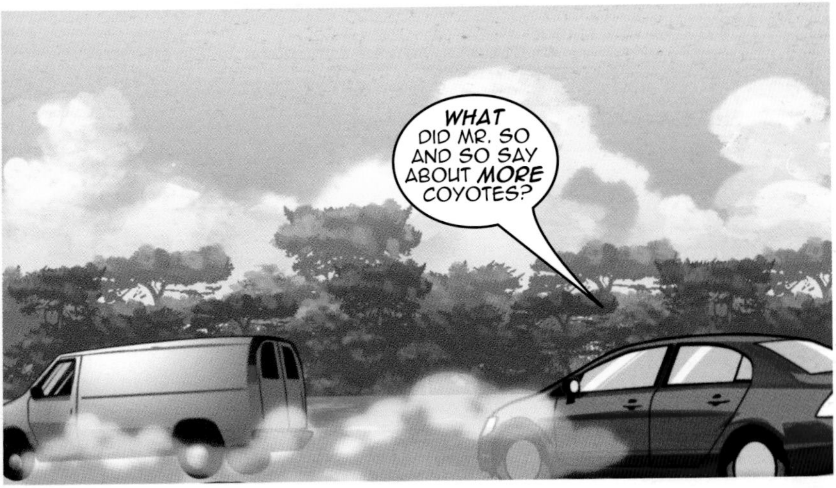
WHAT DID MR. SO AND SO SAY ABOUT MORE COYOTES?

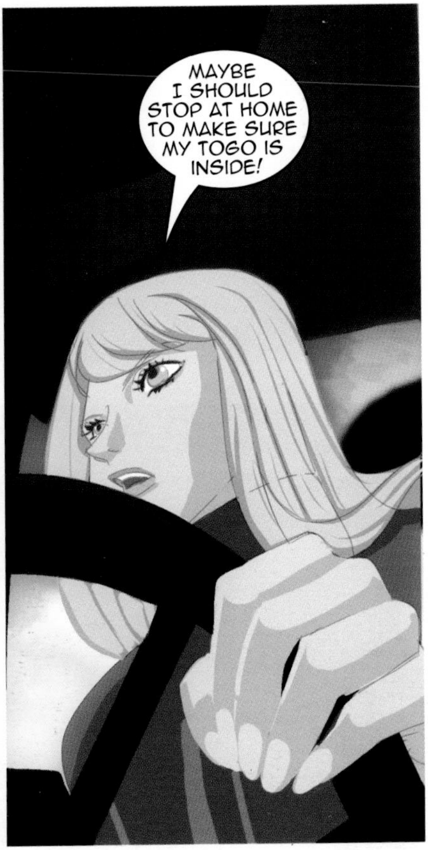
MAYBE I SHOULD STOP AT HOME TO MAKE SURE MY TOGO IS INSIDE!

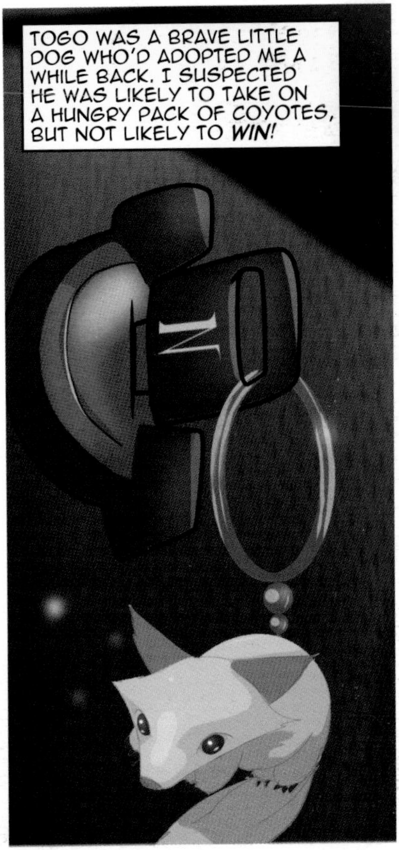
TOGO WAS A BRAVE LITTLE DOG WHO'D ADOPTED ME A WHILE BACK. I SUSPECTED HE WAS LIKELY TO TAKE ON A HUNGRY PACK OF COYOTES, BUT NOT LIKELY TO WIN!

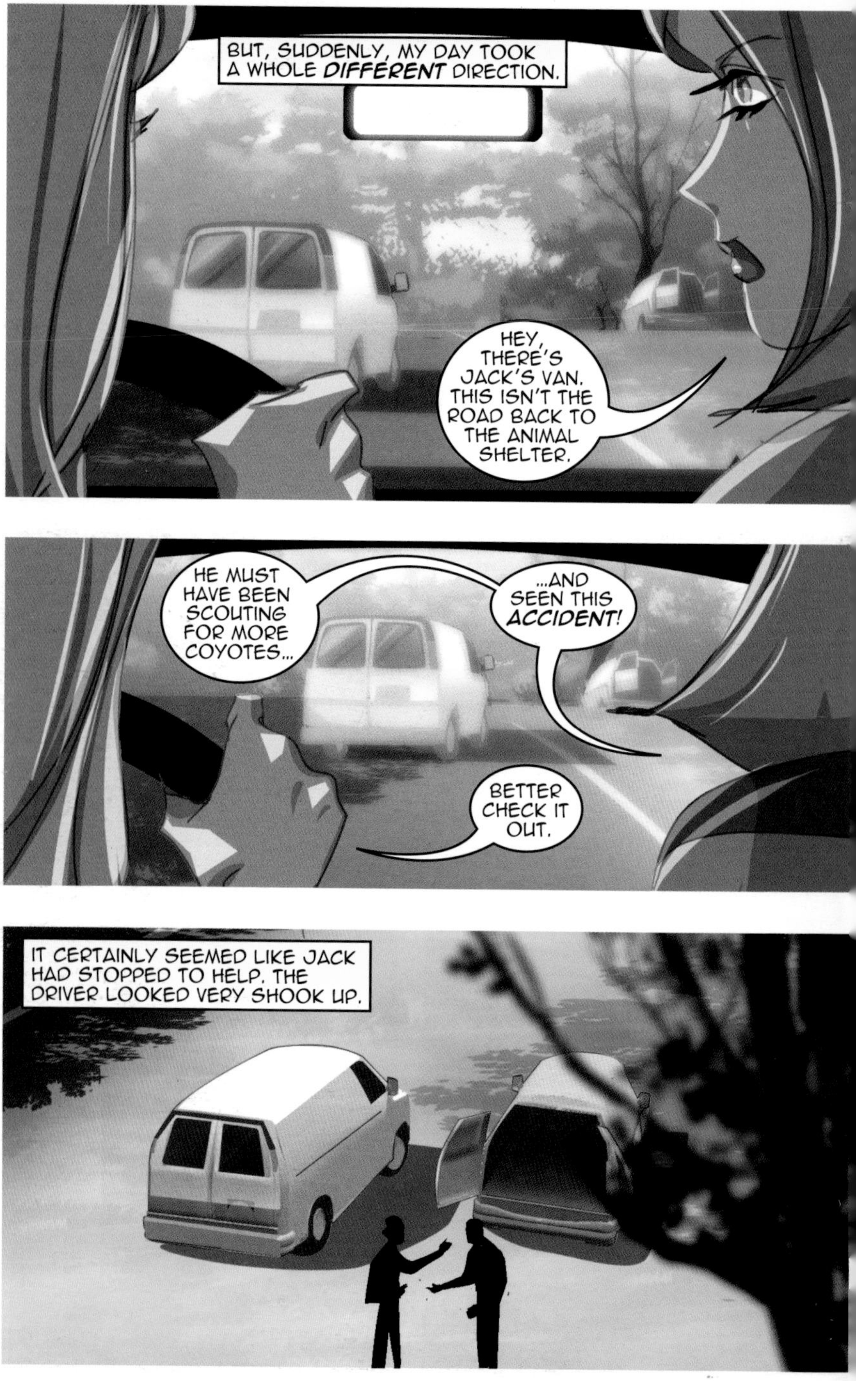
BUT, SUDDENLY, MY DAY TOOK A WHOLE DIFFERENT DIRECTION.
HEY, THERE'S JACK'S VAN. THIS ISN'T THE ROAD BACK TO THE ANIMAL SHELTER.
HE MUST HAVE BEEN SCOUTING FOR MORE COYOTES...
...AND SEEN THIS ACCIDENT!
BETTER CHECK IT OUT.
IT CERTAINLY SEEMED LIKE JACK HAD STOPPED TO HELP. THE DRIVER LOOKED VERY SHOOK UP.

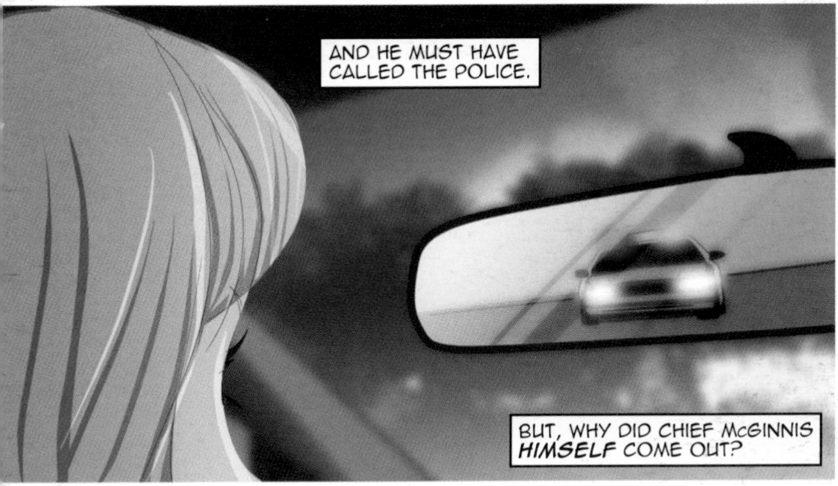
AND HE MUST HAVE CALLED THE POLICE.
BUT, WHY DID CHIEF McGINNIS **HIMSELF** COME OUT?

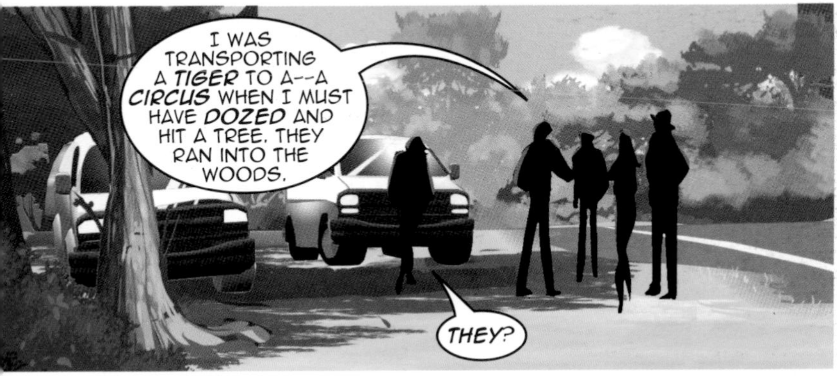
I WAS TRANSPORTING A **TIGER** TO A--A **CIRCUS** WHEN I MUST HAVE **DOZED** AND HIT A TREE. THEY RAN INTO THE WOODS.
THEY?

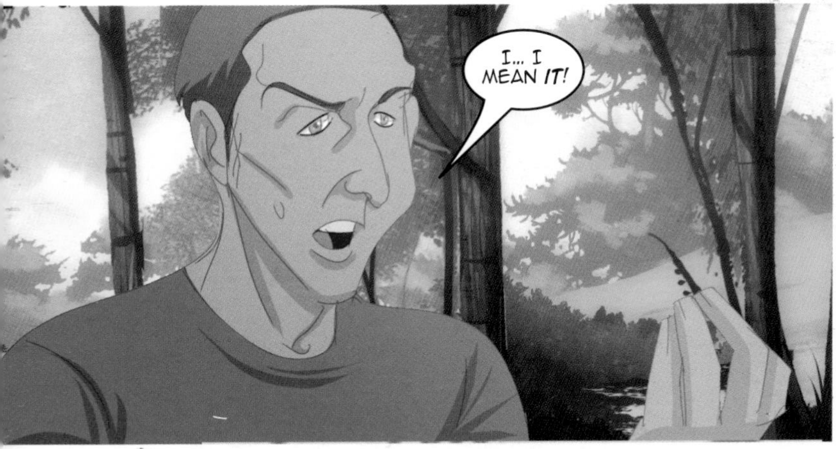
I... I MEAN **IT!**

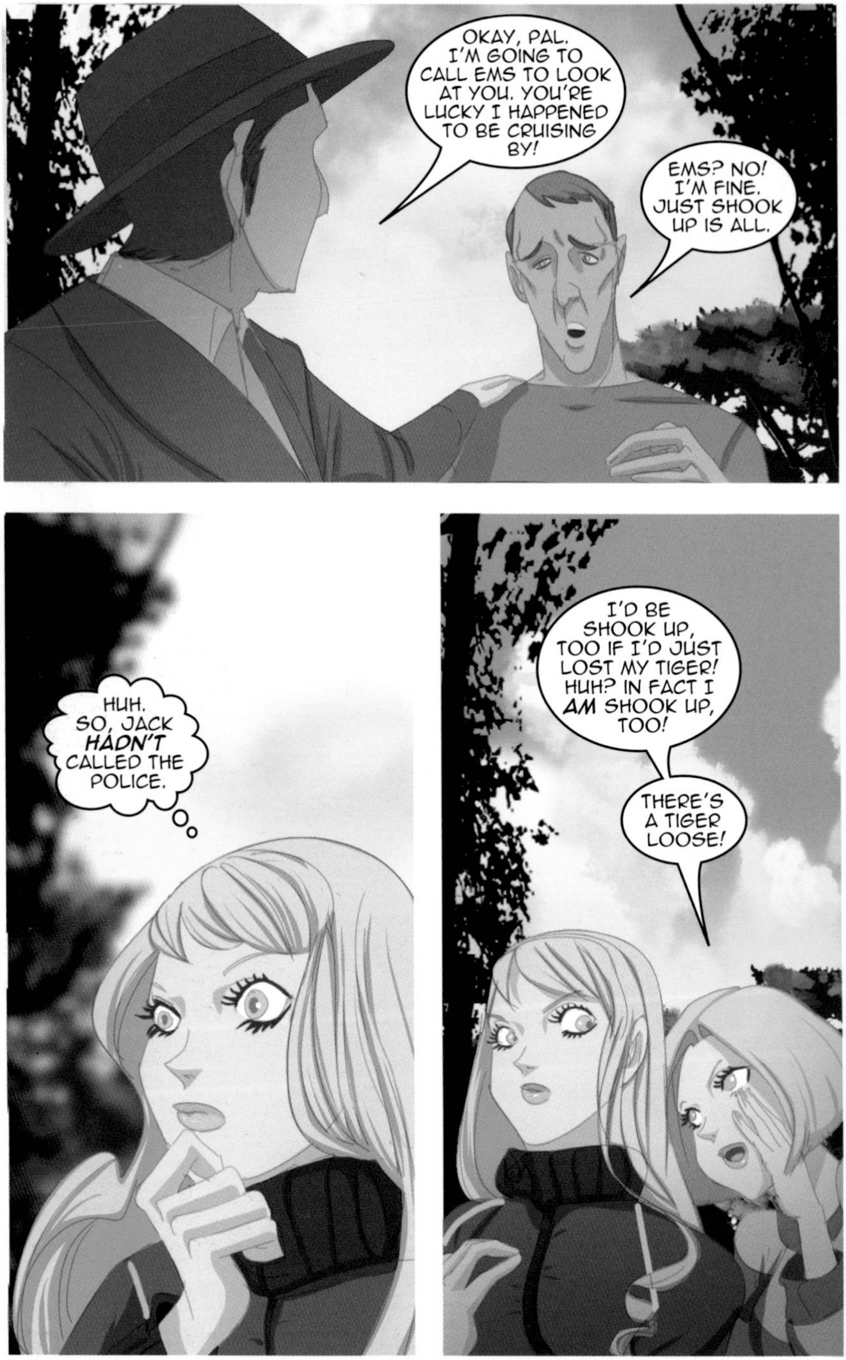
OKAY, PAL. I'M GOING TO CALL EMS TO LOOK AT YOU. YOU'RE LUCKY I HAPPENED TO BE CRUISING BY!
EMS? NO! I'M FINE. JUST SHOOK UP IS ALL.
HUH. SO, JACK HADN'T CALLED THE POLICE.
I'D BE SHOOK UP, TOO IF I'D JUST LOST MY TIGER! HUH? IN FACT I AM SHOOK UP, TOO!
THERE'S A TIGER LOOSE!

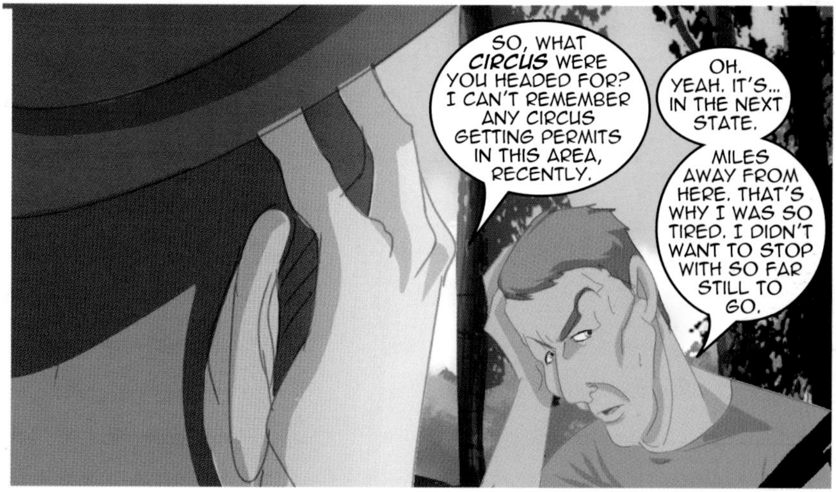
SO, WHAT CIRCUS WERE YOU HEADED FOR? I CAN'T REMEMBER ANY CIRCUS GETTING PERMITS IN THIS AREA, RECENTLY.
OH. YEAH. IT'S... IN THE NEXT STATE.
MILES AWAY FROM HERE. THAT'S WHY I WAS SO TIRED. I DIDN'T WANT TO STOP WITH SO FAR STILL TO GO.

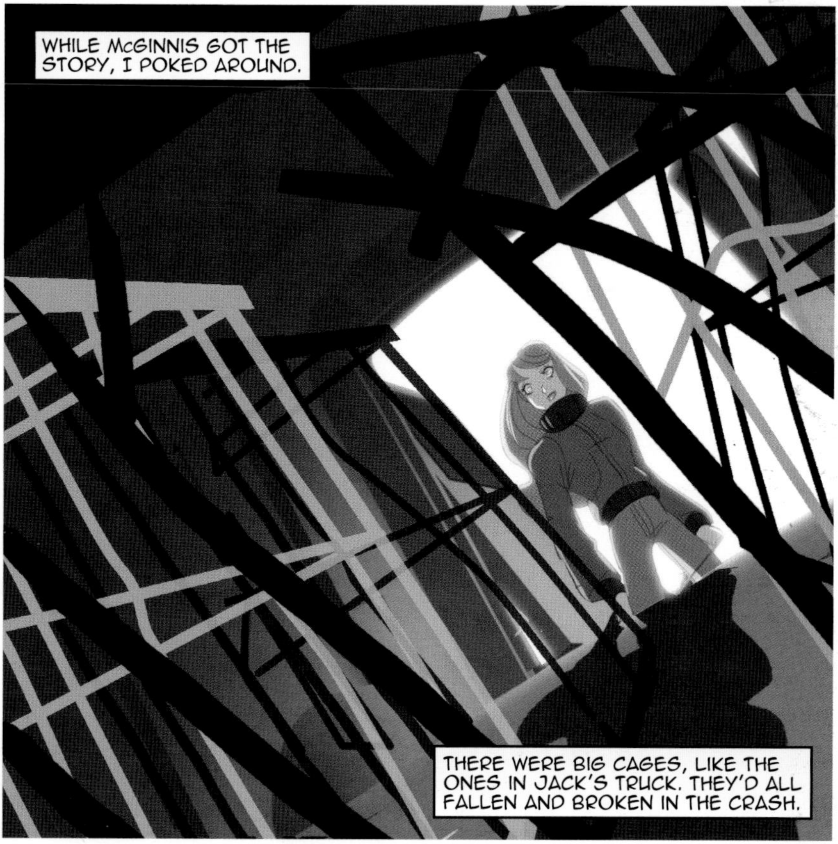
WHILE McGINNIS GOT THE STORY, I POKED AROUND.
THERE WERE BIG CAGES, LIKE THE ONES IN JACK'S TRUCK. THEY'D ALL FALLEN AND BROKEN IN THE CRASH.

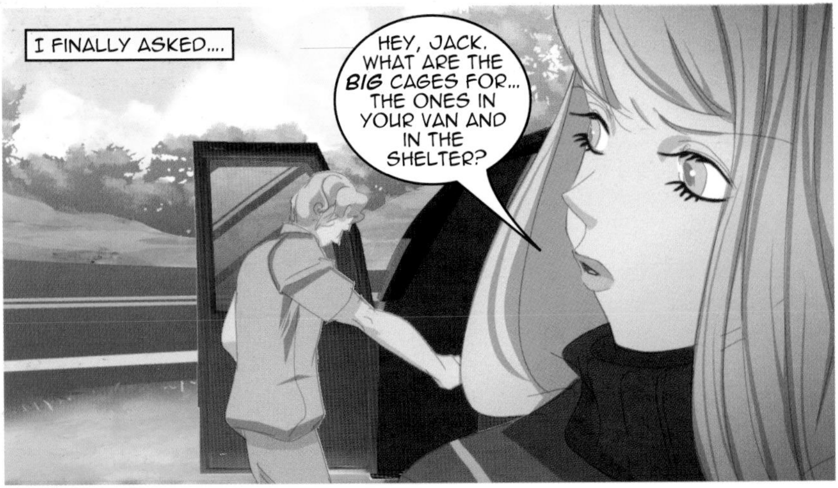
I FINALLY ASKED....
HEY, JACK. WHAT ARE THE *BIG* CAGES FOR... THE ONES IN YOUR VAN AND IN THE SHELTER?

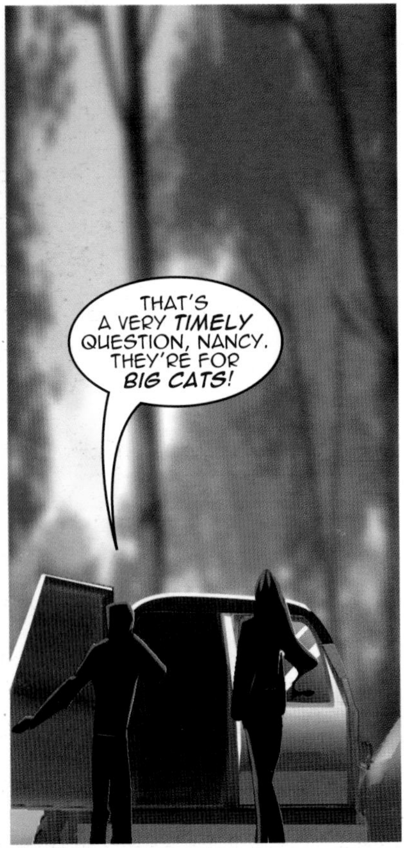
THAT'S A VERY *TIMELY* QUESTION, NANCY. THEY'RE FOR *BIG CATS!*

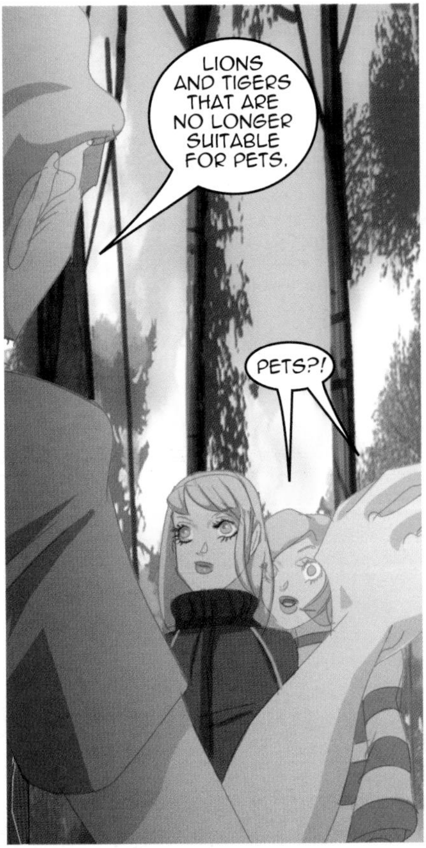
LIONS AND TIGERS THAT ARE NO LONGER SUITABLE FOR PETS.
PETS?!

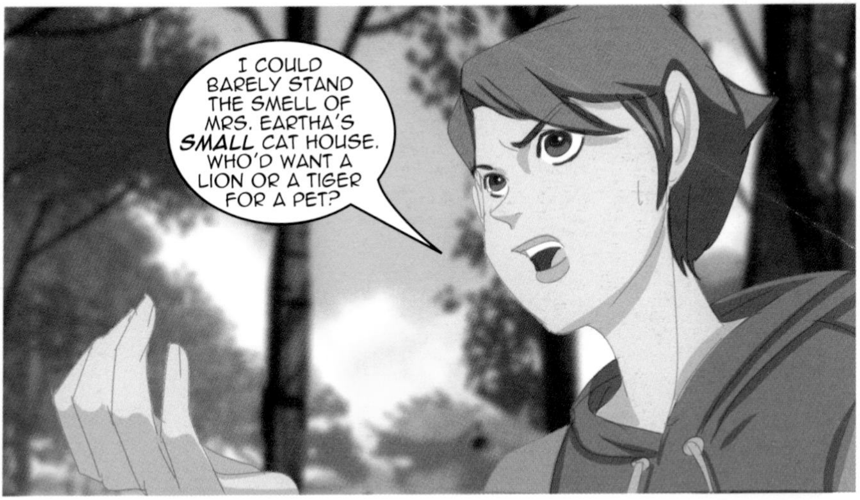
I COULD BARELY STAND THE SMELL OF MRS. EARTHA'S SMALL CAT HOUSE. WHO'D WANT A LION OR A TIGER FOR A PET?

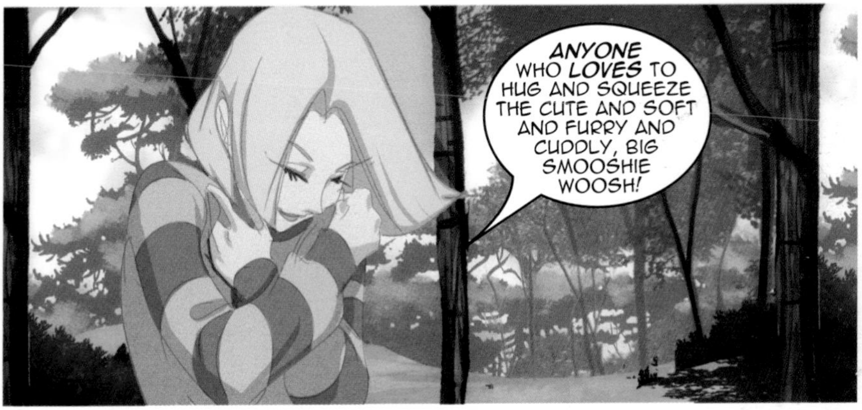
ANYONE WHO LOVES TO HUG AND SQUEEZE THE CUTE AND SOFT AND FURRY AND CUDDLY, BIG SMOOSHIE WOOSH!

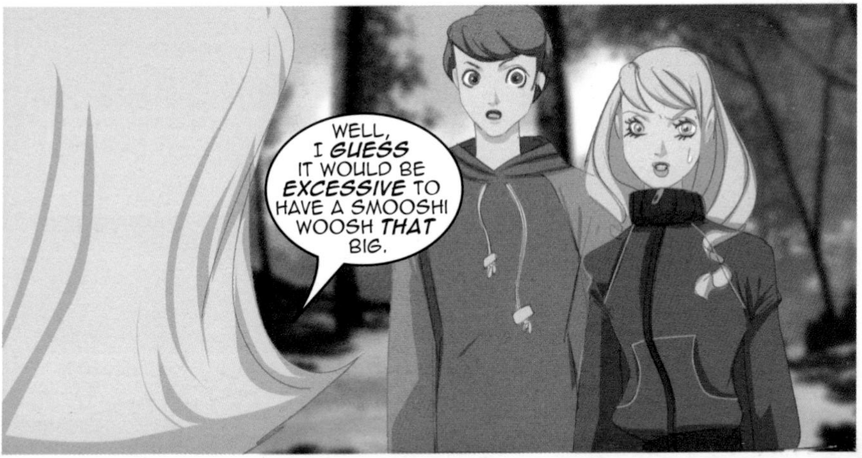
WELL, I GUESS IT WOULD BE EXCESSIVE TO HAVE A SMOOSHI WOOSH THAT BIG.

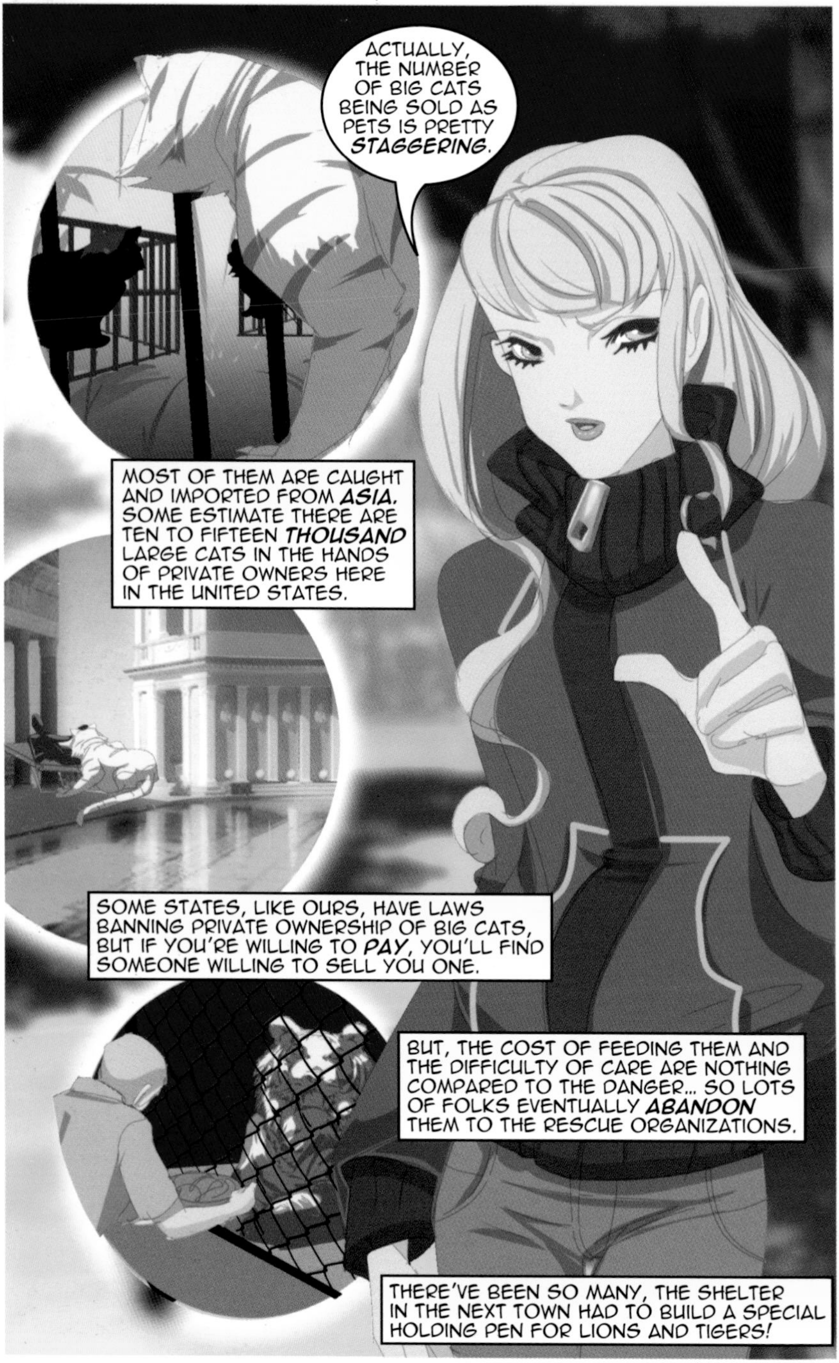
ACTUALLY, THE NUMBER OF BIG CATS BEING SOLD AS PETS IS PRETTY **STAGGERING**.
MOST OF THEM ARE CAUGHT AND IMPORTED FROM **ASIA.** SOME ESTIMATE THERE ARE TEN TO FIFTEEN **THOUSAND** LARGE CATS IN THE HANDS OF PRIVATE OWNERS HERE IN THE UNITED STATES.
SOME STATES, LIKE OURS, HAVE LAWS BANNING PRIVATE OWNERSHIP OF BIG CATS, BUT IF YOU'RE WILLING TO **PAY**, YOU'LL FIND SOMEONE WILLING TO SELL YOU ONE.
BUT, THE COST OF FEEDING THEM AND THE DIFFICULTY OF CARE ARE NOTHING COMPARED TO THE DANGER... SO LOTS OF FOLKS EVENTUALLY **ABANDON** THEM TO THE RESCUE ORGANIZATIONS.
THERE'VE BEEN SO MANY, THE SHELTER IN THE NEXT TOWN HAD TO BUILD A SPECIAL HOLDING PEN FOR LIONS AND TIGERS!

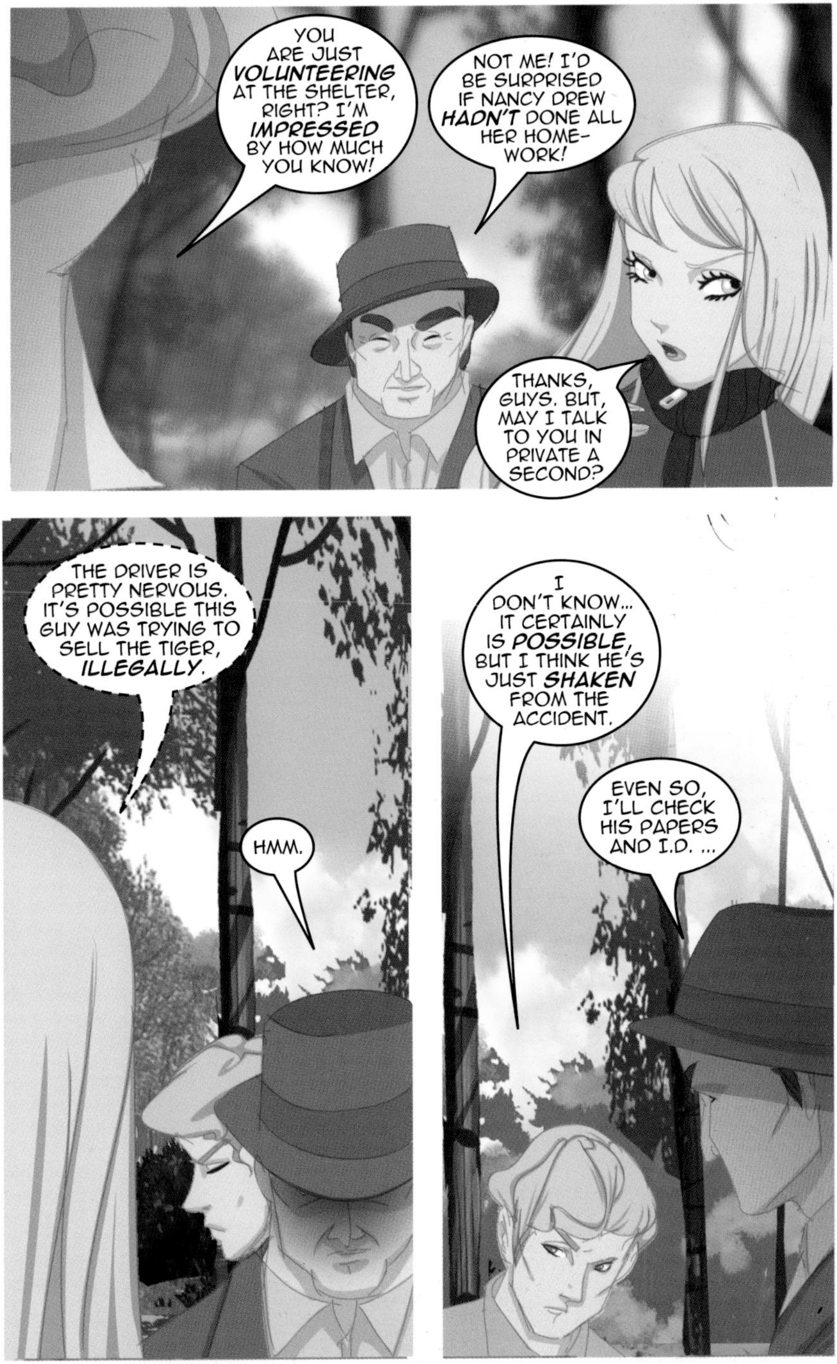
YOU ARE JUST VOLUNTEERING AT THE SHELTER, RIGHT? I'M IMPRESSED BY HOW MUCH YOU KNOW!
NOT ME! I'D BE SURPRISED IF NANCY DREW HADN'T DONE ALL HER HOME-WORK!
THANKS, GUYS. BUT, MAY I TALK TO YOU IN PRIVATE A SECOND?
THE DRIVER IS PRETTY NERVOUS. IT'S POSSIBLE THIS GUY WAS TRYING TO SELL THE TIGER, ILLEGALLY.
HMM.
I DON'T KNOW... IT CERTAINLY IS POSSIBLE, BUT I THINK HE'S JUST SHAKEN FROM THE ACCIDENT.
EVEN SO, I'LL CHECK HIS PAPERS AND I.D. ...

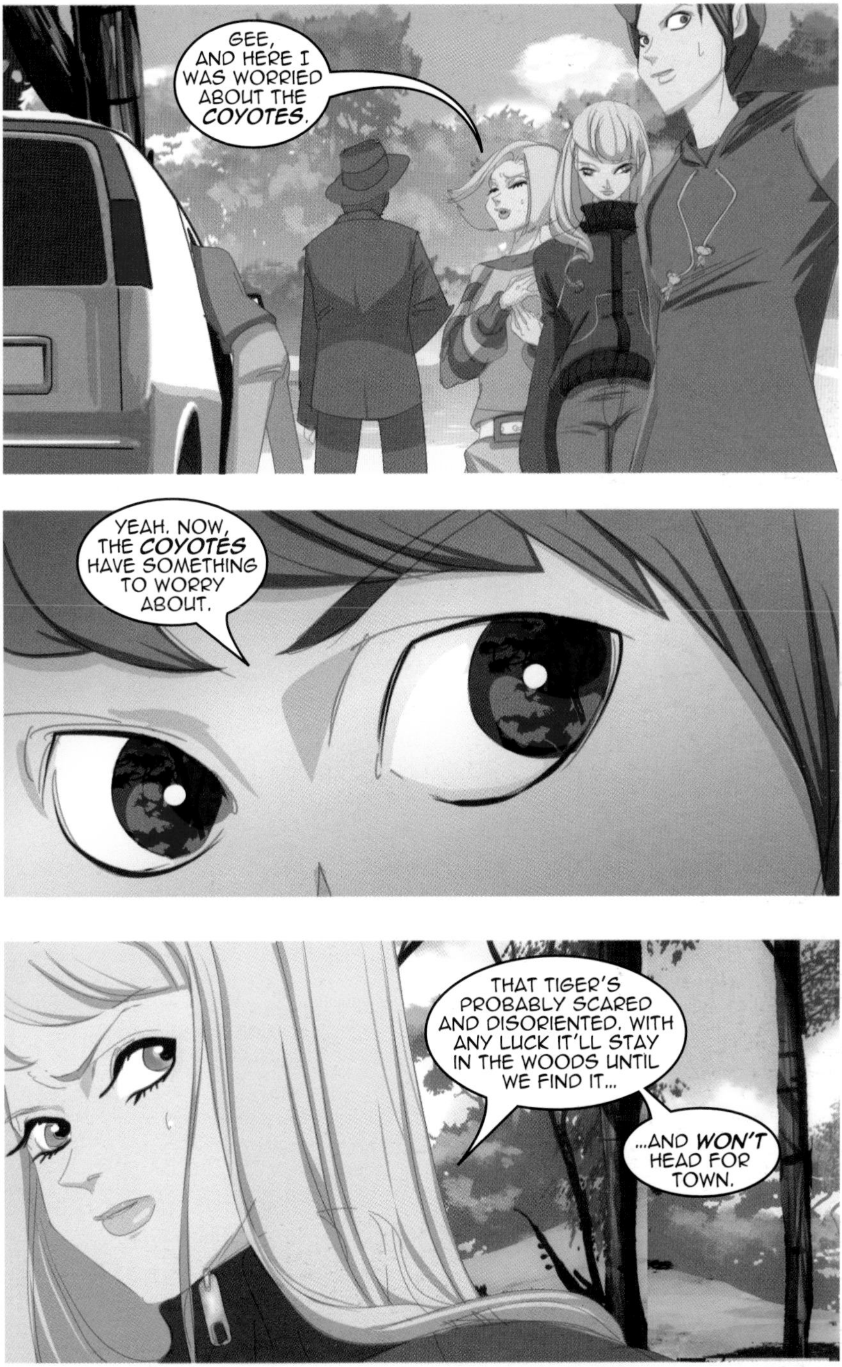
GEE, AND HERE I WAS WORRIED ABOUT THE COYOTES.
YEAH. NOW, THE COYOTES HAVE SOMETHING TO WORRY ABOUT.
THAT TIGER'S PROBABLY SCARED AND DISORIENTED. WITH ANY LUCK IT'LL STAY IN THE WOODS UNTIL WE FIND IT...
...AND WON'T HEAD FOR TOWN.

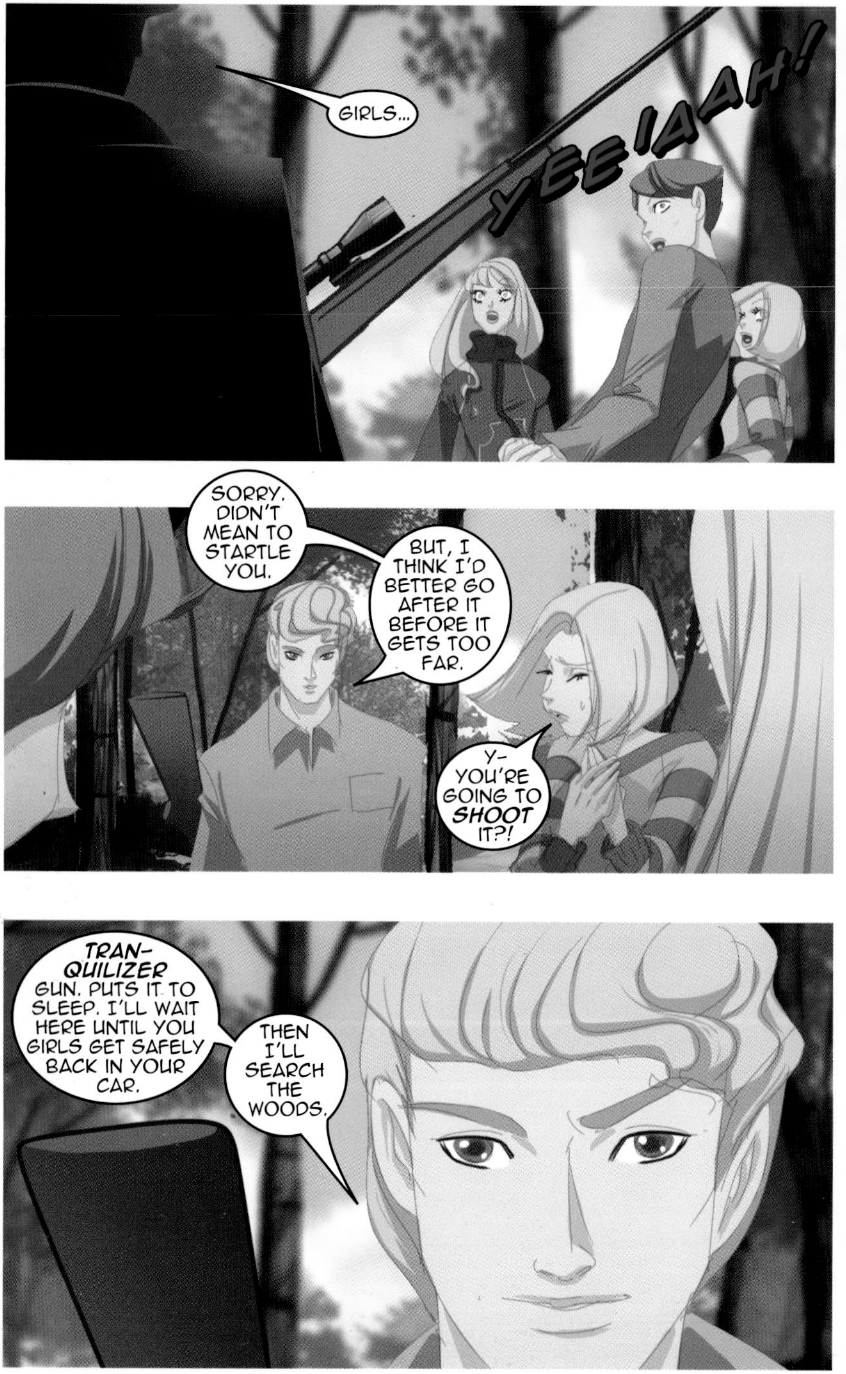
GIRLS...
YEEIAAH!
SORRY. DIDN'T MEAN TO STARTLE YOU.
BUT, I THINK I'D BETTER GO AFTER IT BEFORE IT GETS TOO FAR.
Y-YOU'RE GOING TO SHOOT IT?!
TRAN-QUILIZER GUN. PUTS IT TO SLEEP. I'LL WAIT HERE UNTIL YOU GIRLS GET SAFELY BACK IN YOUR CAR.
THEN I'LL SEARCH THE WOODS.

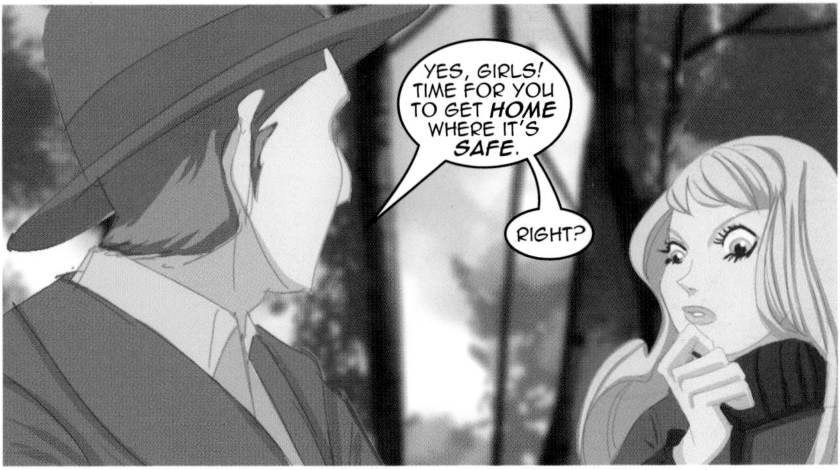
YES, GIRLS! TIME FOR YOU TO GET **HOME** WHERE IT'S **SAFE**.
RIGHT?

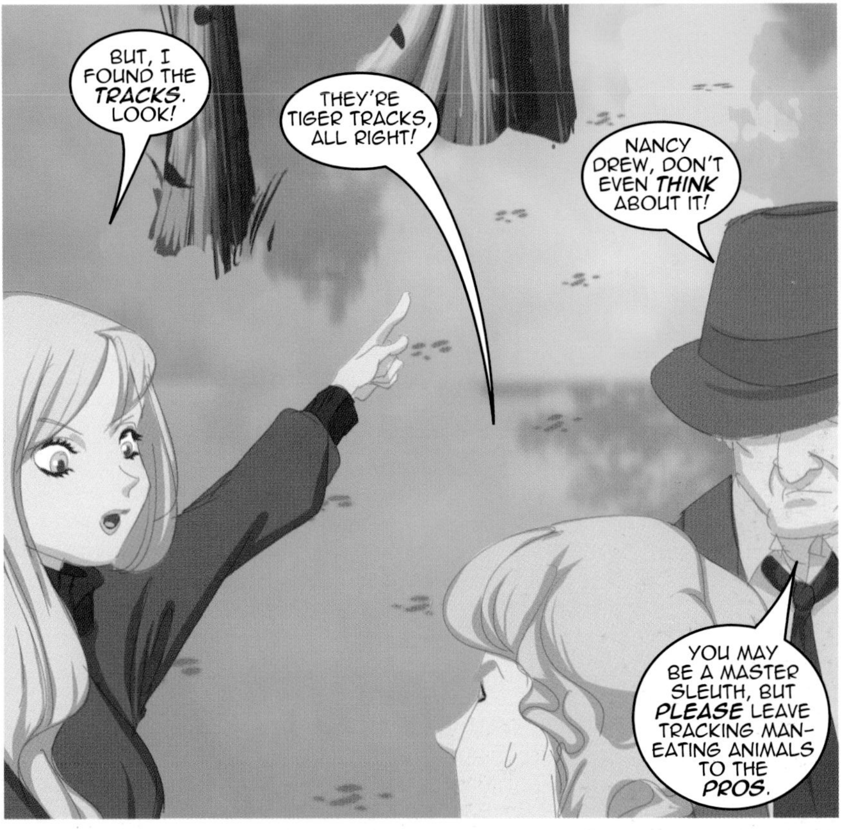
BUT, I FOUND THE **TRACKS**. LOOK!
THEY'RE TIGER TRACKS, ALL RIGHT!
NANCY DREW, DON'T EVEN **THINK** ABOUT IT!
YOU MAY BE A MASTER SLEUTH, BUT **PLEASE** LEAVE TRACKING MAN-EATING ANIMALS TO THE **PROS**.

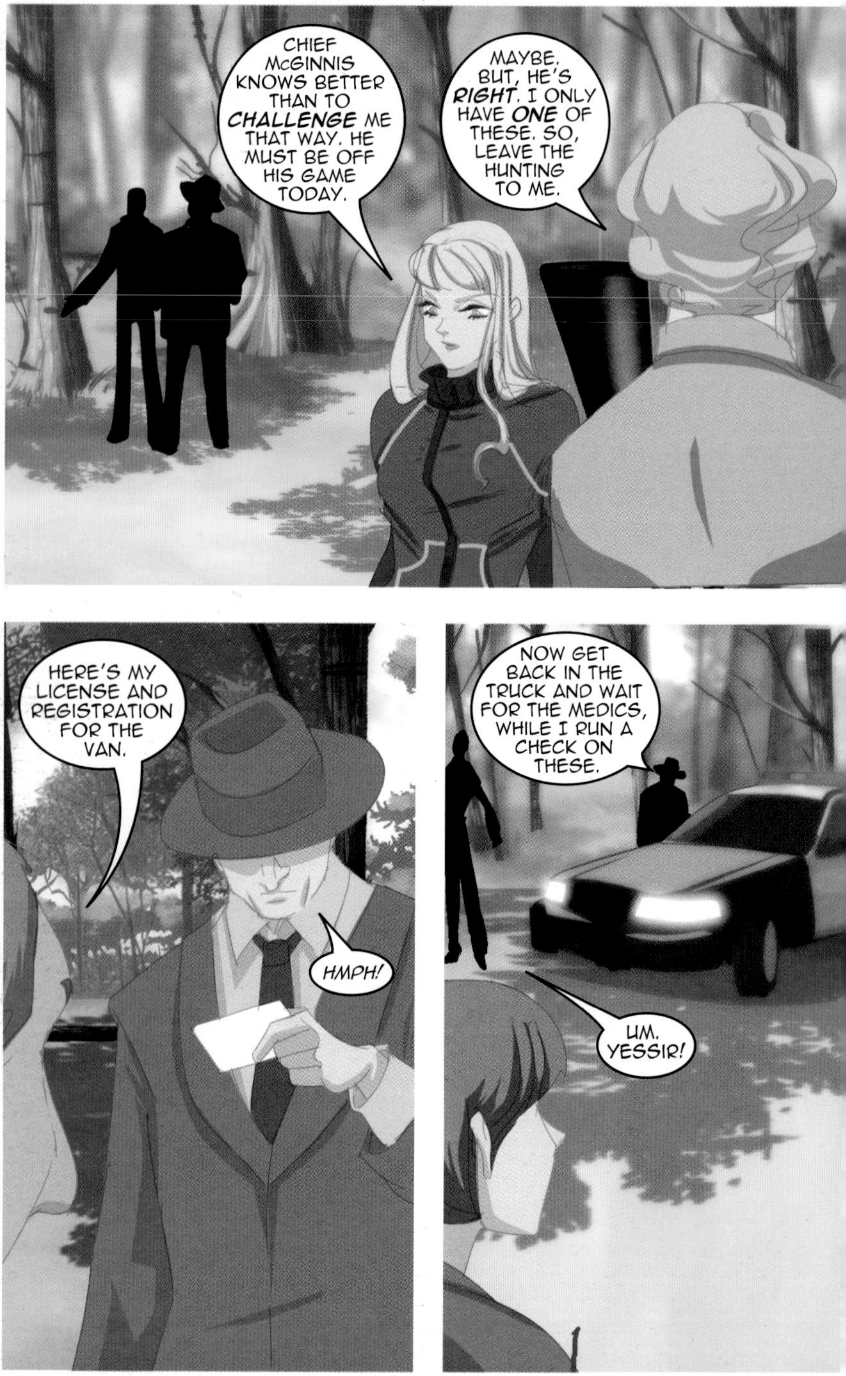
CHIEF McGINNIS KNOWS BETTER THAN TO CHALLENGE ME THAT WAY. HE MUST BE OFF HIS GAME TODAY.
MAYBE. BUT, HE'S RIGHT. I ONLY HAVE ONE OF THESE. SO, LEAVE THE HUNTING TO ME.
HERE'S MY LICENSE AND REGISTRATION FOR THE VAN.
HMPH!
NOW GET BACK IN THE TRUCK AND WAIT FOR THE MEDICS, WHILE I RUN A CHECK ON THESE.
UM. YESSIR!

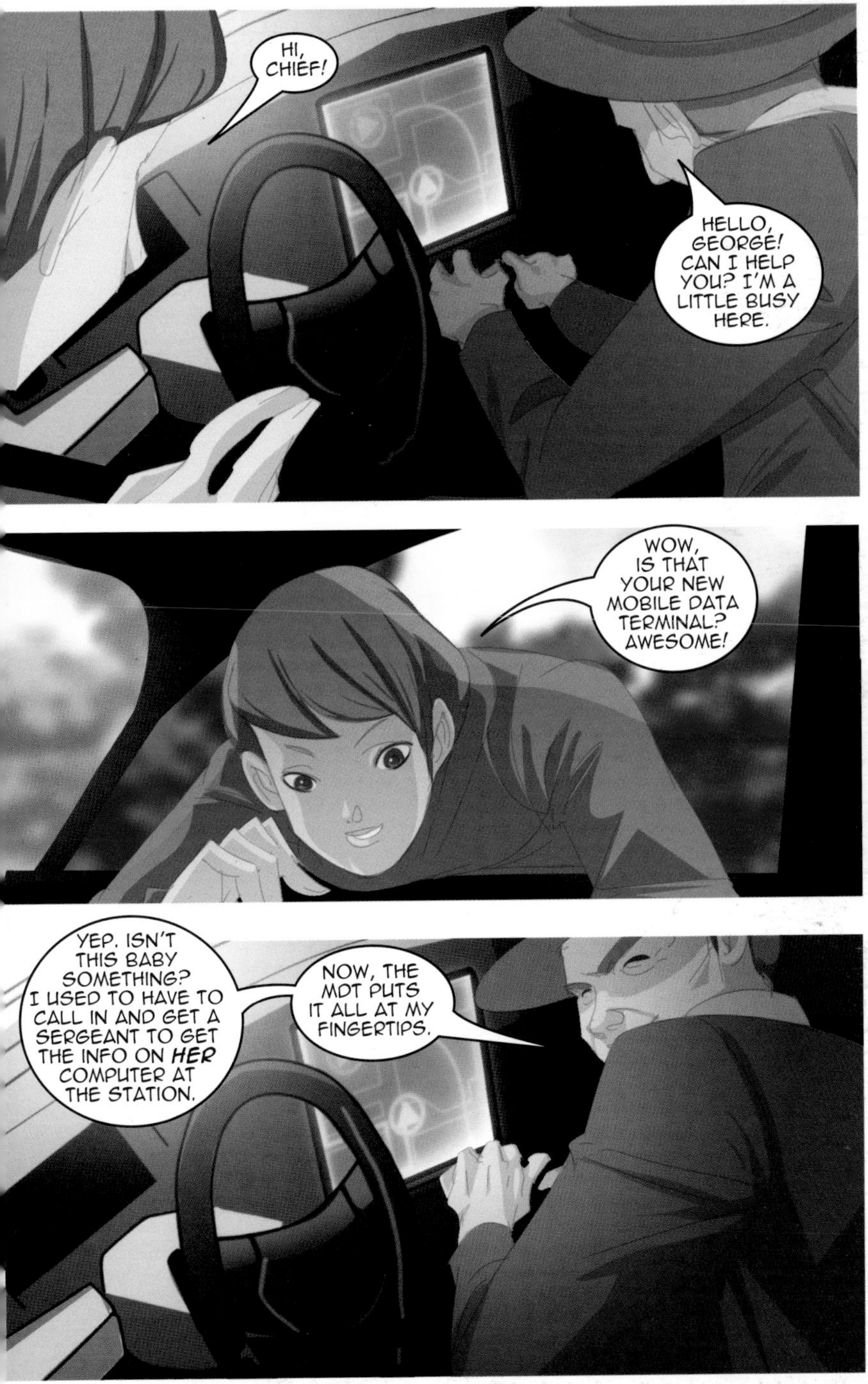
HI, CHIEF!
HELLO, GEORGE! CAN I HELP YOU? I'M A LITTLE BUSY HERE.
WOW, IS THAT YOUR NEW MOBILE DATA TERMINAL? AWESOME!
YEP. ISN'T THIS BABY SOMETHING? I USED TO HAVE TO CALL IN AND GET A SERGEANT TO GET THE INFO ON *HER* COMPUTER AT THE STATION.
NOW, THE MDT PUTS IT ALL AT MY FINGERTIPS.

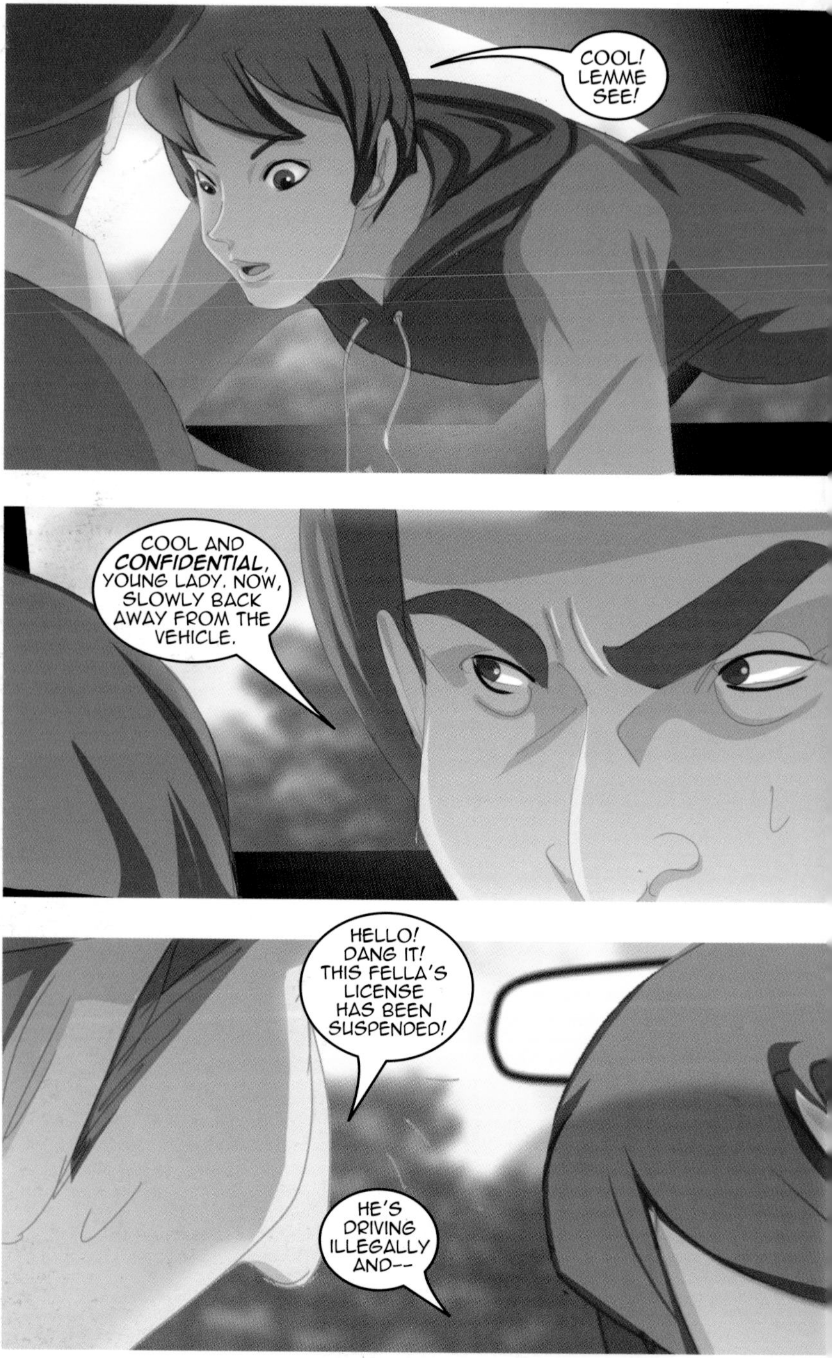
COOL! LEMME SEE!
COOL AND *CONFIDENTIAL*, YOUNG LADY. NOW, SLOWLY BACK AWAY FROM THE VEHICLE.
HELLO! DANG IT! THIS FELLA'S LICENSE HAS BEEN SUSPENDED!
HE'S DRIVING ILLEGALLY AND--

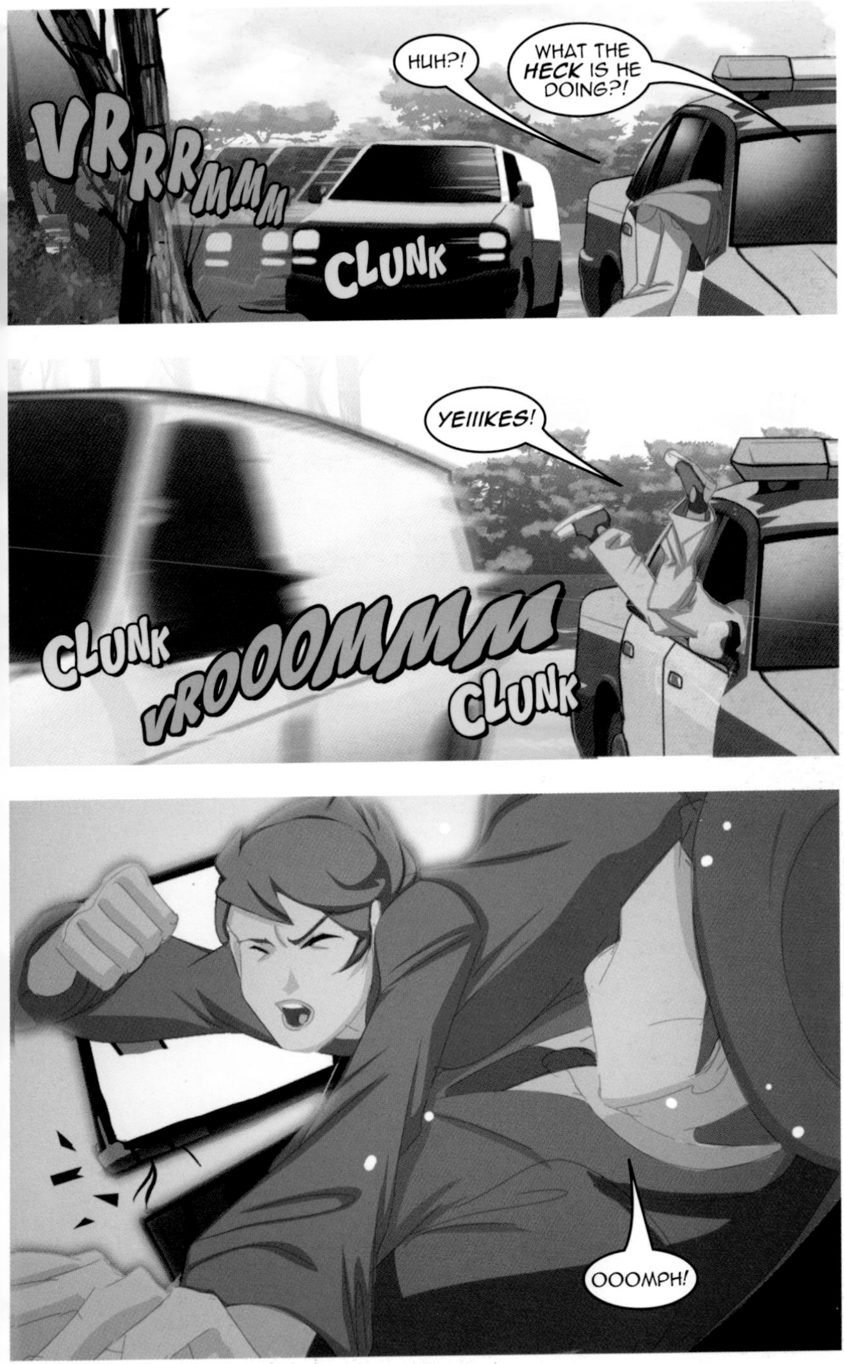
VRRRMMM
CLUNK
HUH?!
WHAT THE HECK IS HE DOING?!
YEIIIKES!
CLUNK
VROOOMMMM
CLUNK
OOOMPH!

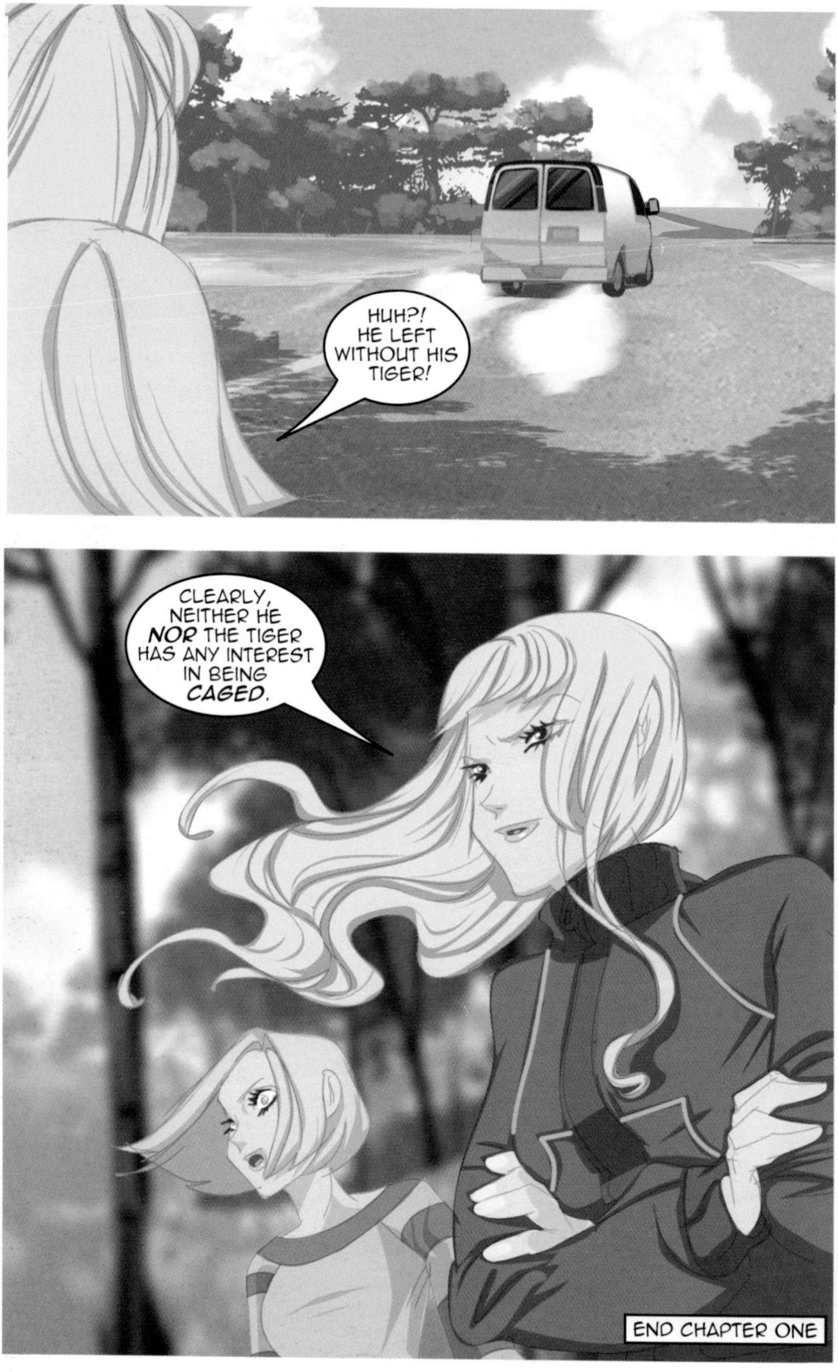
HUH?! HE LEFT WITHOUT HIS TIGER!
CLEARLY, NEITHER HE NOR THE TIGER HAS ANY INTEREST IN BEING CAGED.
END CHAPTER ONE

UNFORTUNATELY, A HIGH-SPEED CHASE WASN'T POSSIBLE WHILE CHIEF McGINNIS HAD A CIVILIAN PASSENGER WHO'D, UH, *DROPPED IN*.
HE'S GETTING AWAY!
OUT OF THE CAR, GEORGE! *NOW!*
CHAPTER TWO: TIGER WOODS

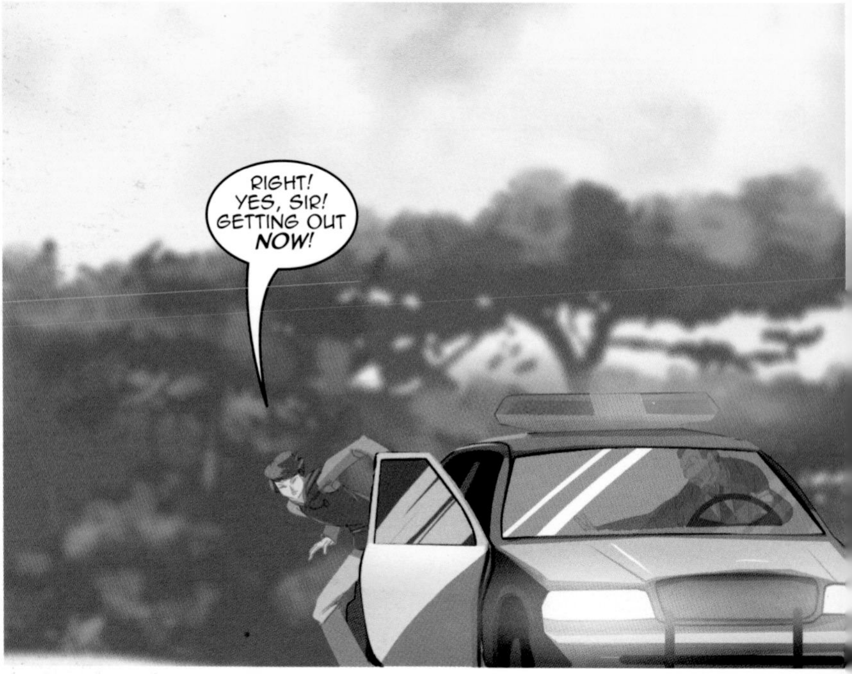
RIGHT! YES, SIR! GETTING OUT NOW!

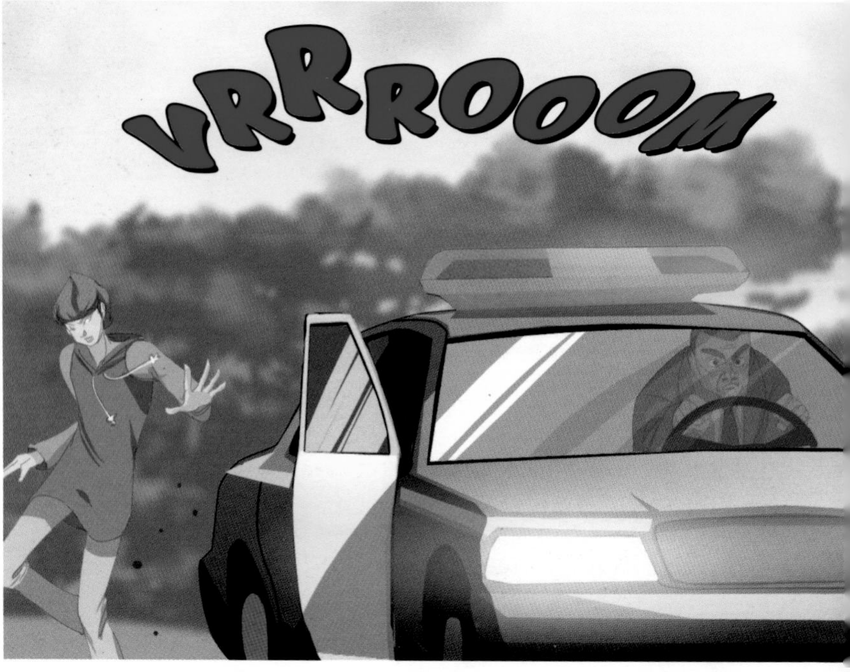
VRRROOOM

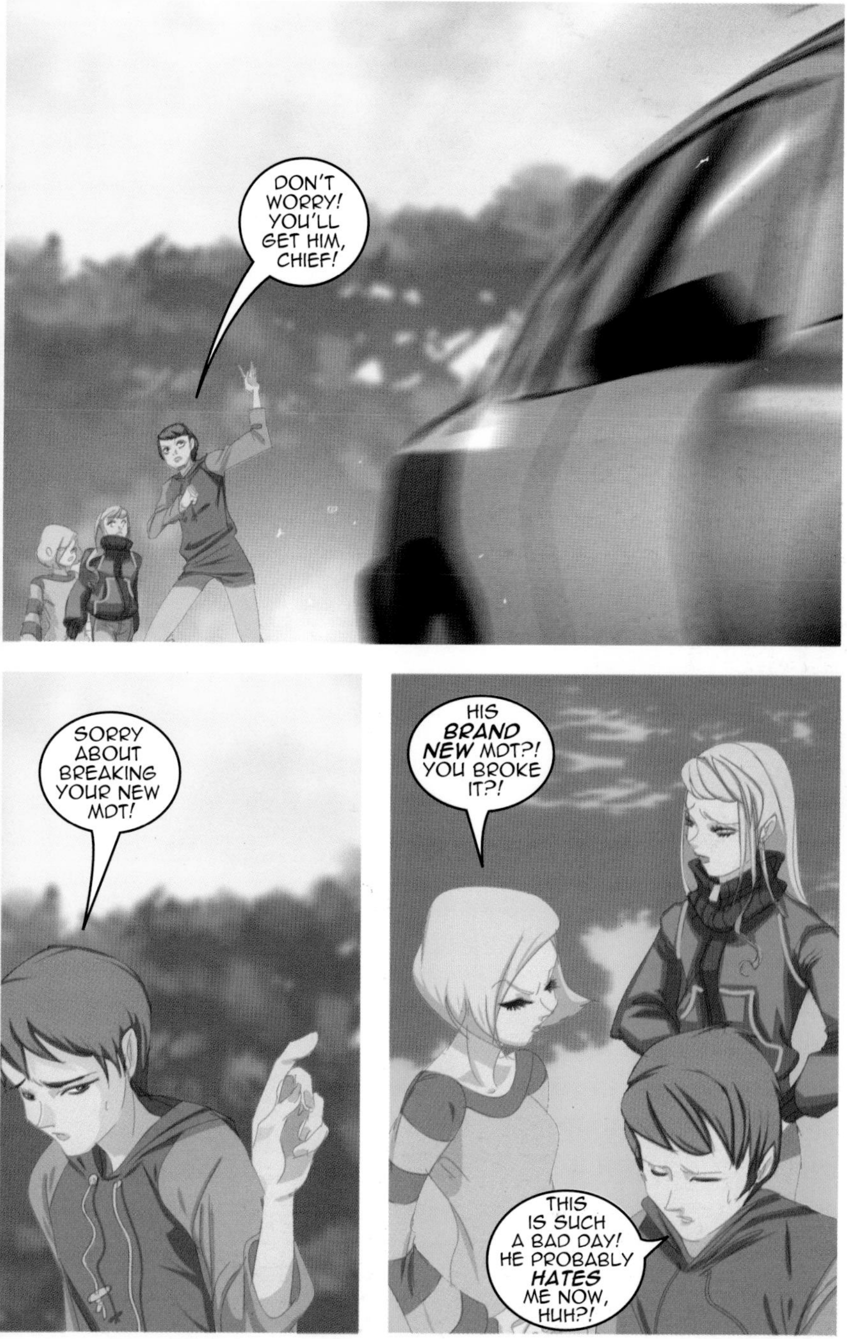
DON'T WORRY! YOU'LL GET HIM, CHIEF!
SORRY ABOUT BREAKING YOUR NEW MDT!
HIS **BRAND NEW** MDT?! YOU BROKE IT?!
THIS IS SUCH A BAD DAY! HE PROBABLY **HATES** ME NOW, HUH?!

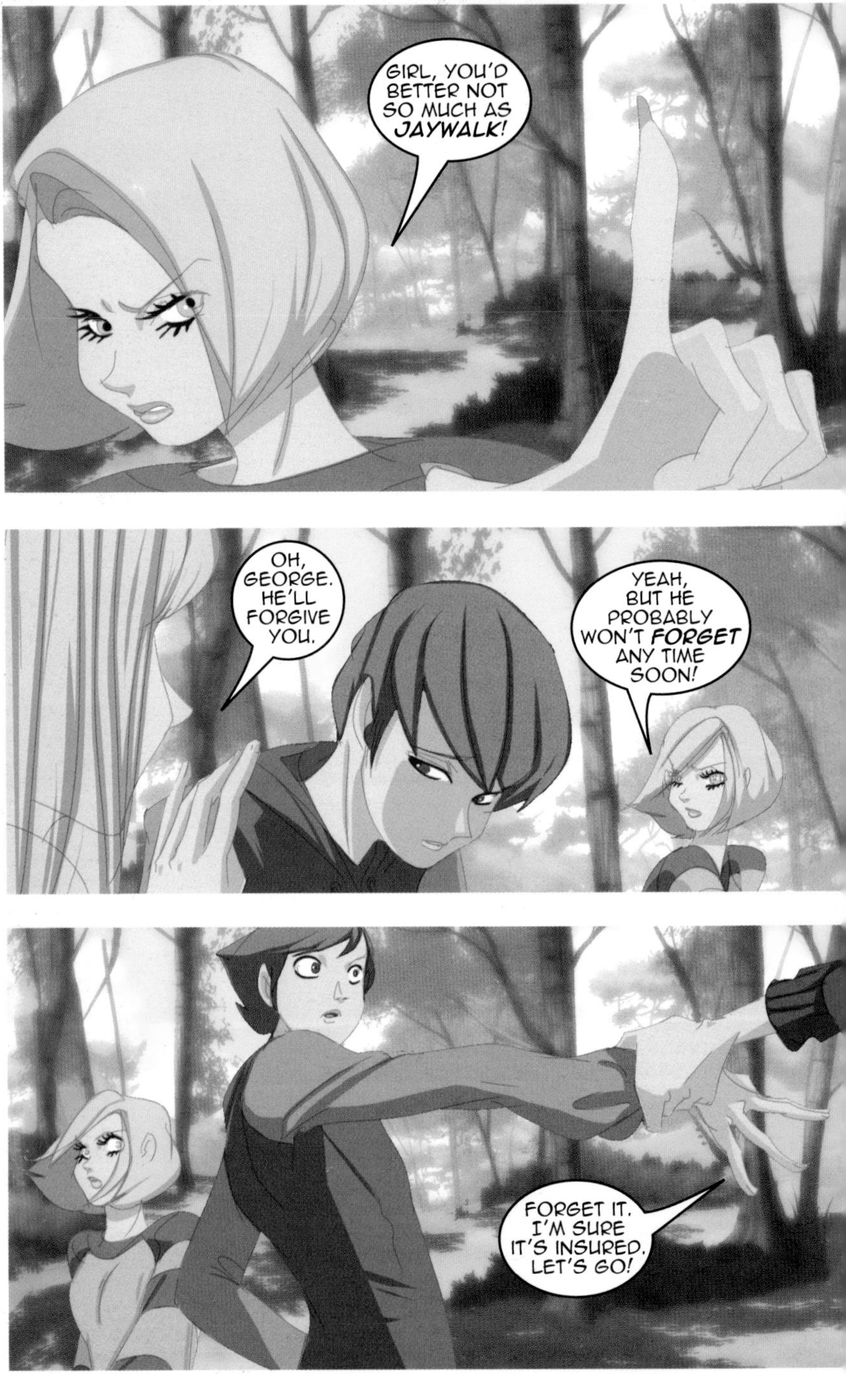
GIRL, YOU'D BETTER NOT SO MUCH AS JAYWALK!
OH, GEORGE. HE'LL FORGIVE YOU.
YEAH, BUT HE PROBABLY WON'T FORGET ANY TIME SOON!
FORGET IT. I'M SURE IT'S INSURED. LET'S GO!

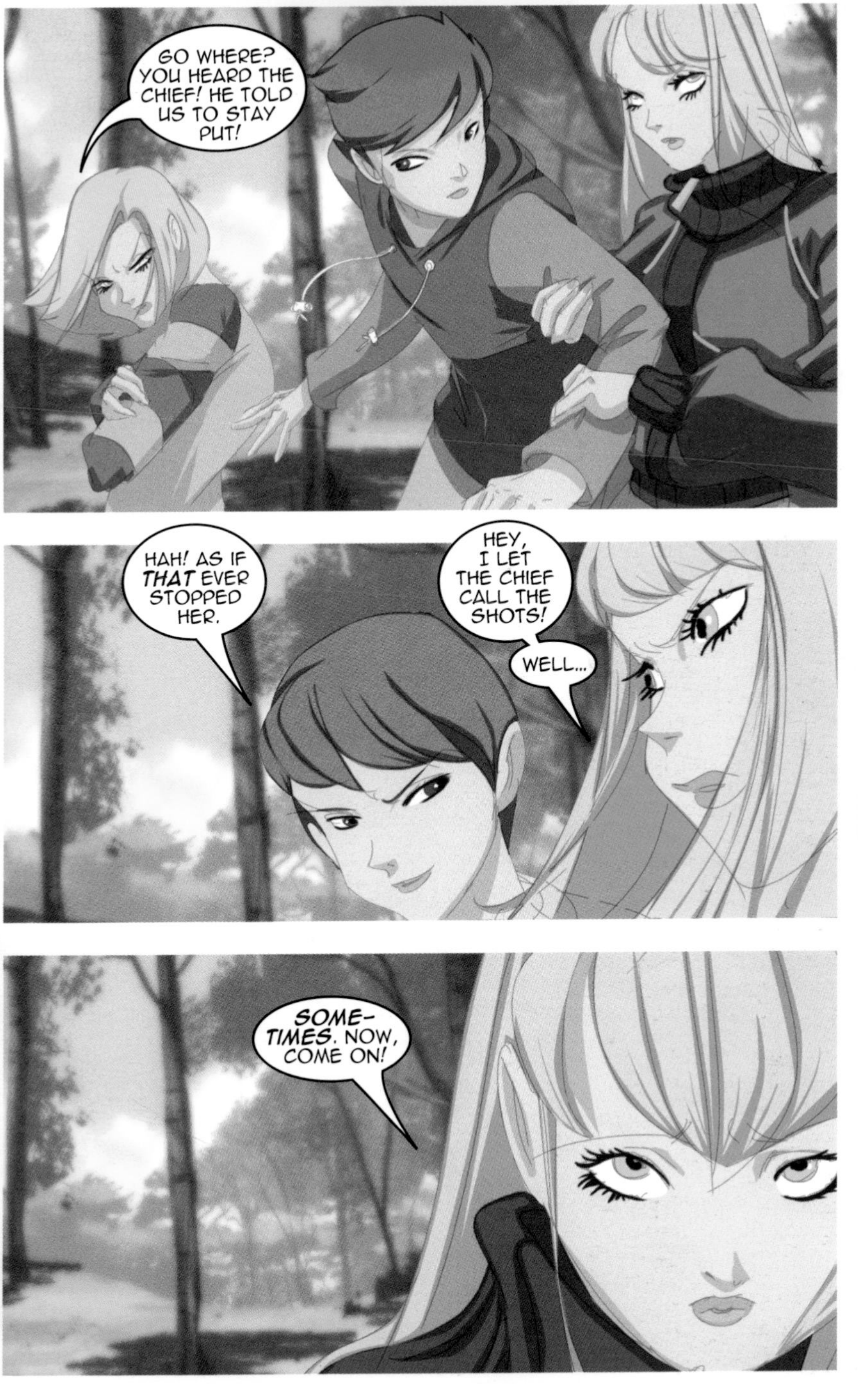
GO WHERE? YOU HEARD THE CHIEF! HE TOLD US TO STAY PUT!
HAH! AS IF *THAT* EVER STOPPED HER.
HEY, I LET THE CHIEF CALL THE SHOTS!
WELL...
SOME-TIMES. NOW, COME ON!

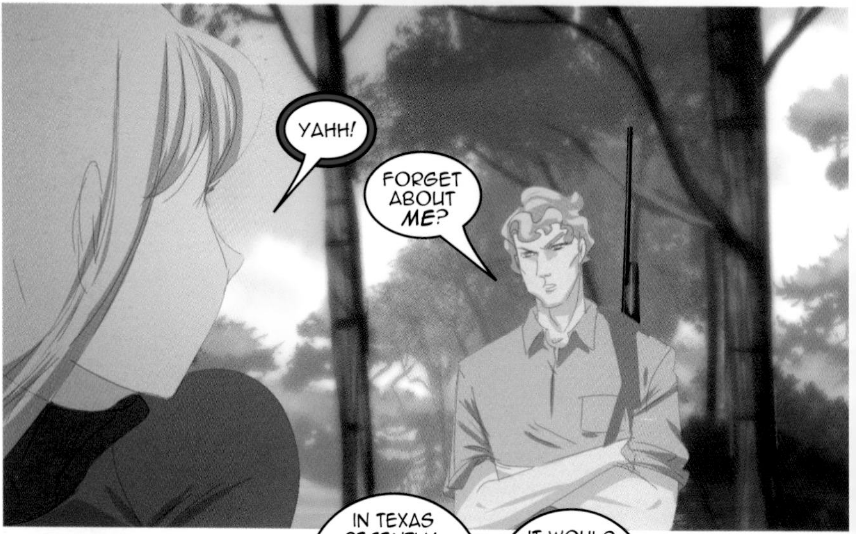
YAHH!
FORGET ABOUT *ME*?

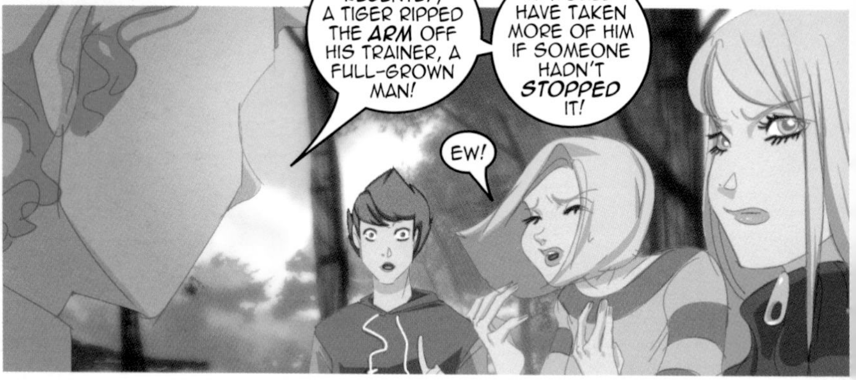
IN TEXAS RECENTLY, A TIGER RIPPED THE *ARM* OFF HIS TRAINER, A FULL-GROWN MAN!
IT WOULD HAVE TAKEN MORE OF HIM IF SOMEONE HADN'T *STOPPED* IT!
EW!

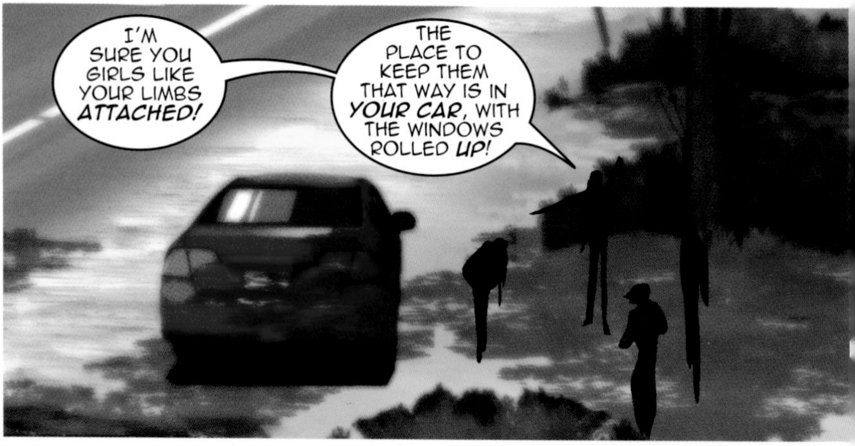
I'M SURE YOU GIRLS LIKE YOUR LIMBS *ATTACHED!*
THE PLACE TO KEEP THEM THAT WAY IS IN *YOUR CAR*, WITH THE WINDOWS ROLLED *UP*!

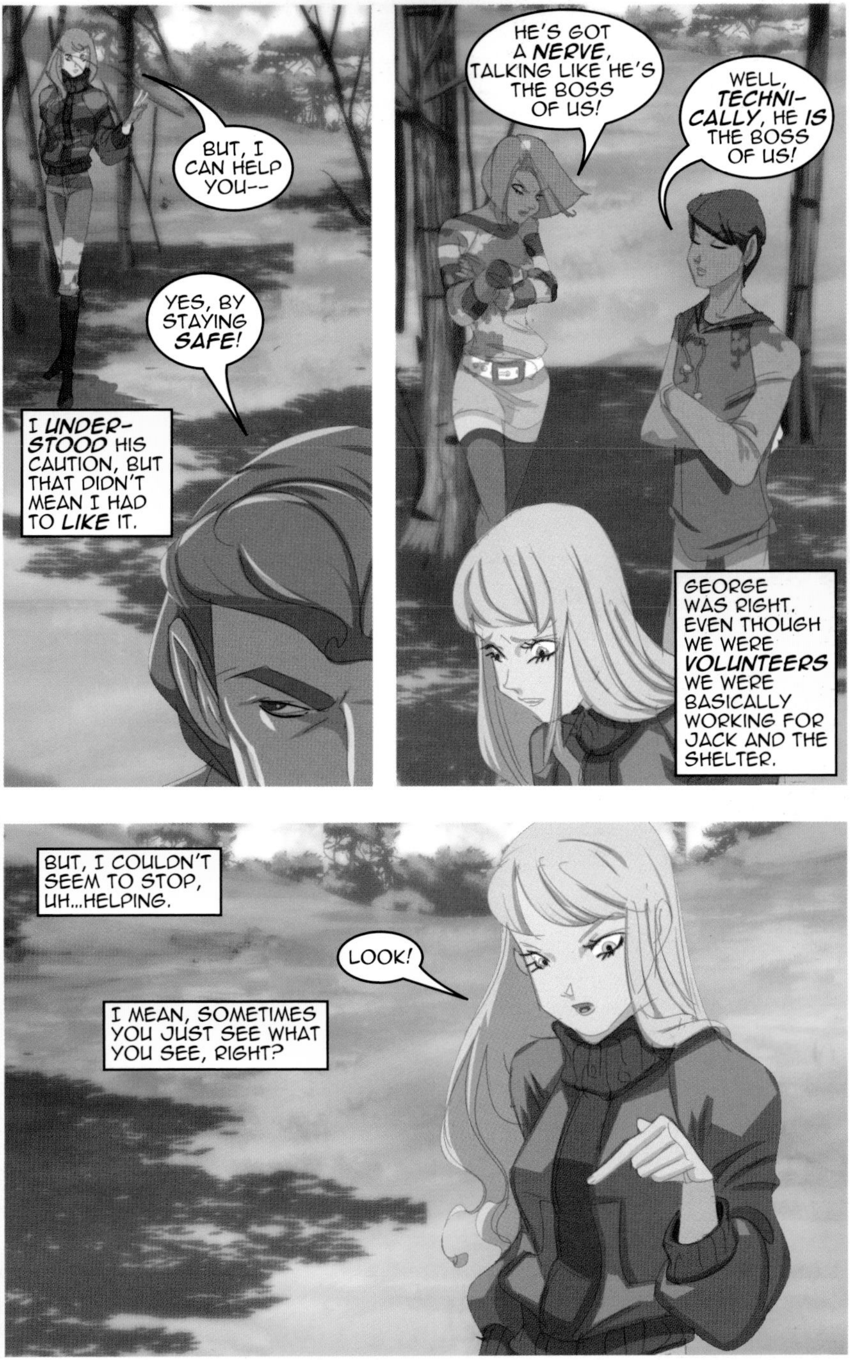
BUT, I CAN HELP YOU--
YES, BY STAYING SAFE!
I UNDERSTOOD HIS CAUTION, BUT THAT DIDN'T MEAN I HAD TO LIKE IT.
HE'S GOT A NERVE, TALKING LIKE HE'S THE BOSS OF US!
WELL, TECHNICALLY, HE IS THE BOSS OF US!
GEORGE WAS RIGHT. EVEN THOUGH WE WERE VOLUNTEERS WE WERE BASICALLY WORKING FOR JACK AND THE SHELTER.
BUT, I COULDN'T SEEM TO STOP, UH...HELPING.
LOOK!
I MEAN, SOMETIMES YOU JUST SEE WHAT YOU SEE, RIGHT?

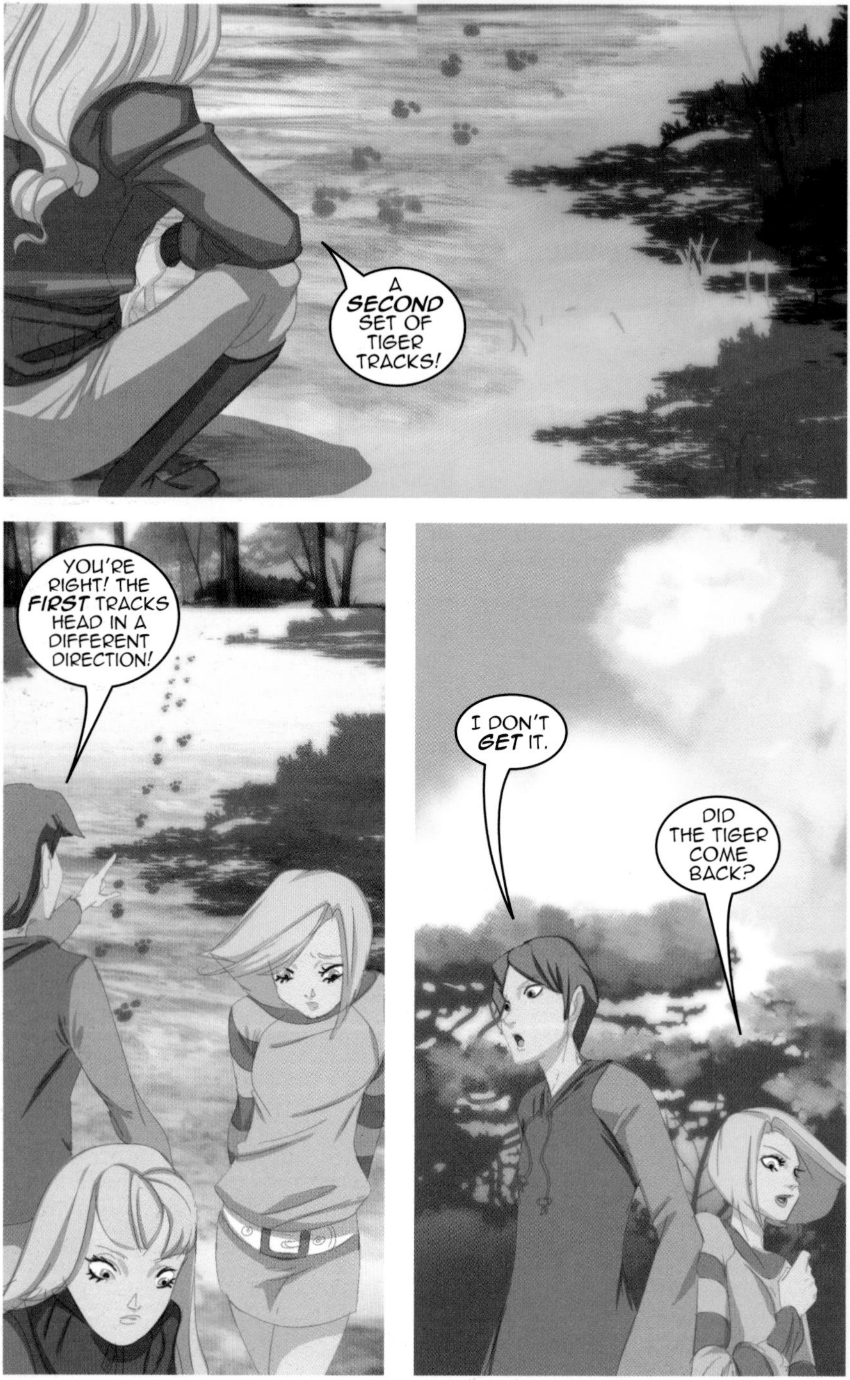
A SECOND SET OF TIGER TRACKS!
YOU'RE RIGHT! THE FIRST TRACKS HEAD IN A DIFFERENT DIRECTION!
I DON'T GET IT.
DID THE TIGER COME BACK?

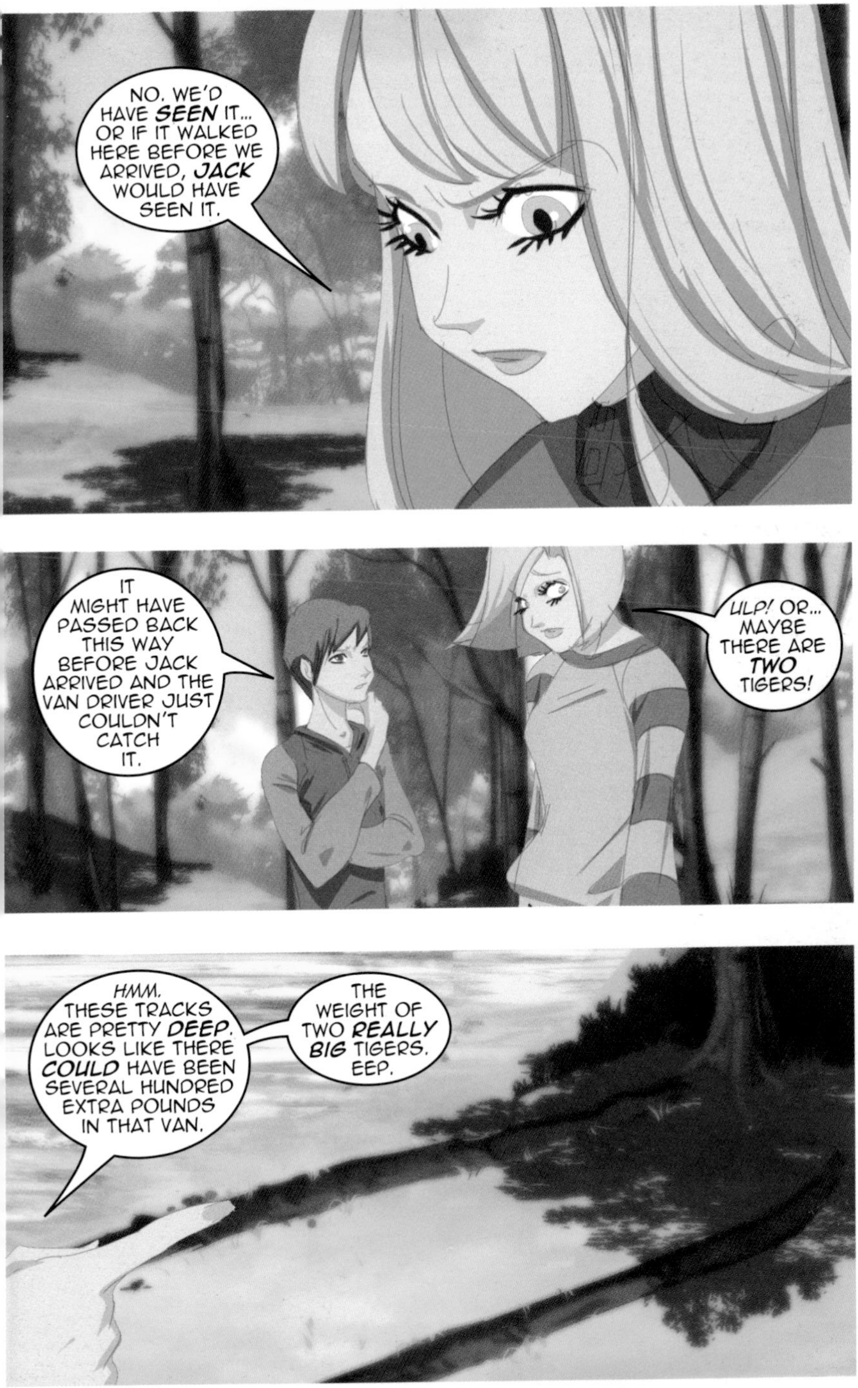
NO. WE'D HAVE SEEN IT... OR IF IT WALKED HERE BEFORE WE ARRIVED, JACK WOULD HAVE SEEN IT.
IT MIGHT HAVE PASSED BACK THIS WAY BEFORE JACK ARRIVED AND THE VAN DRIVER JUST COULDN'T CATCH IT.
ULP! OR... MAYBE THERE ARE TWO TIGERS!
HMM. THESE TRACKS ARE PRETTY DEEP. LOOKS LIKE THERE COULD HAVE BEEN SEVERAL HUNDRED EXTRA POUNDS IN THAT VAN.
THE WEIGHT OF TWO REALLY BIG TIGERS. EEP.

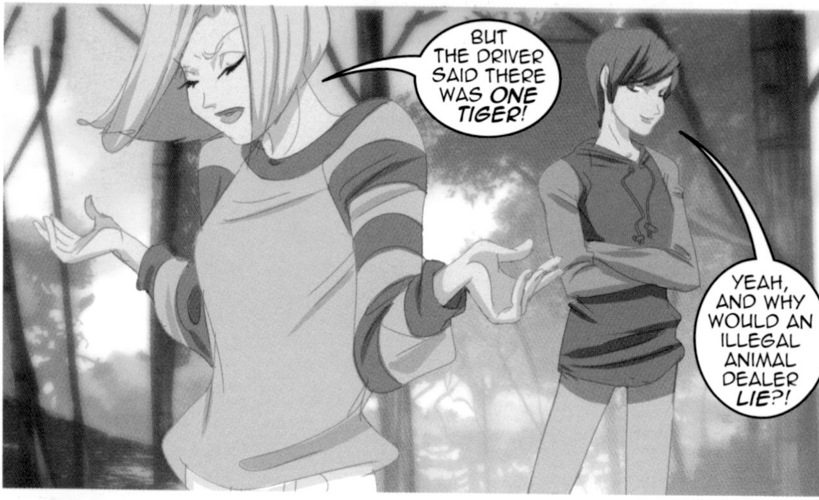
BUT THE DRIVER SAID THERE WAS ONE TIGER!
YEAH, AND WHY WOULD AN ILLEGAL ANIMAL DEALER LIE?!

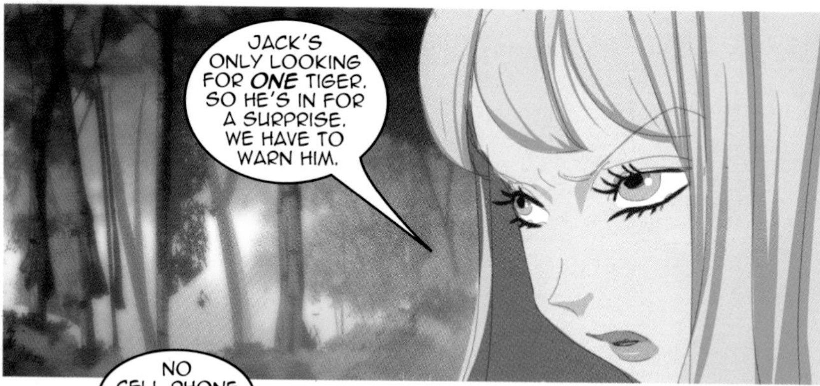
JACK'S ONLY LOOKING FOR ONE TIGER, SO HE'S IN FOR A SURPRISE. WE HAVE TO WARN HIM.

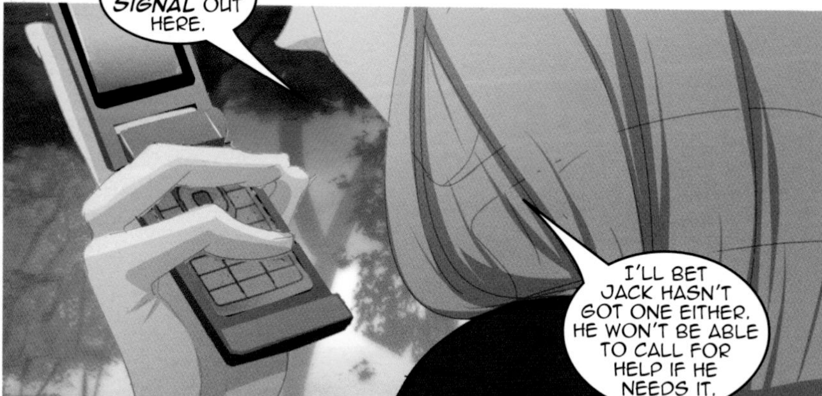
NO CELL PHONE SIGNAL OUT HERE.
I'LL BET JACK HASN'T GOT ONE EITHER. HE WON'T BE ABLE TO CALL FOR HELP IF HE NEEDS IT.

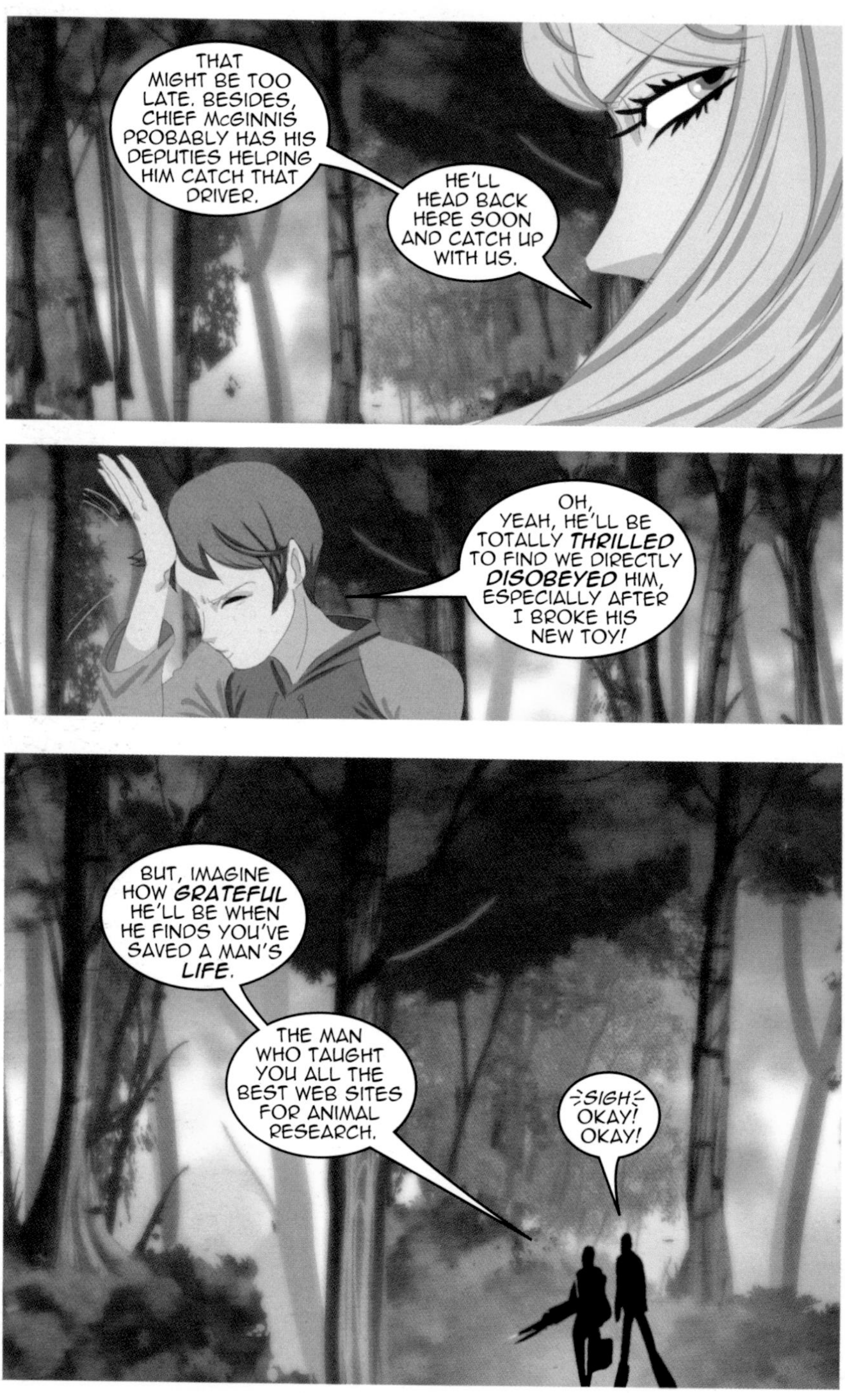
THAT MIGHT BE TOO LATE. BESIDES, CHIEF McGINNIS PROBABLY HAS HIS DEPUTIES HELPING HIM CATCH THAT DRIVER.
HE'LL HEAD BACK HERE SOON AND CATCH UP WITH US.
OH, YEAH, HE'LL BE TOTALLY *THRILLED* TO FIND WE DIRECTLY *DISOBEYED* HIM, ESPECIALLY AFTER I BROKE HIS NEW TOY!
BUT, IMAGINE HOW *GRATEFUL* HE'LL BE WHEN HE FINDS YOU'VE SAVED A MAN'S *LIFE*.
THE MAN WHO TAUGHT YOU ALL THE BEST WEB SITES FOR ANIMAL RESEARCH.
SIGH OKAY! OKAY!

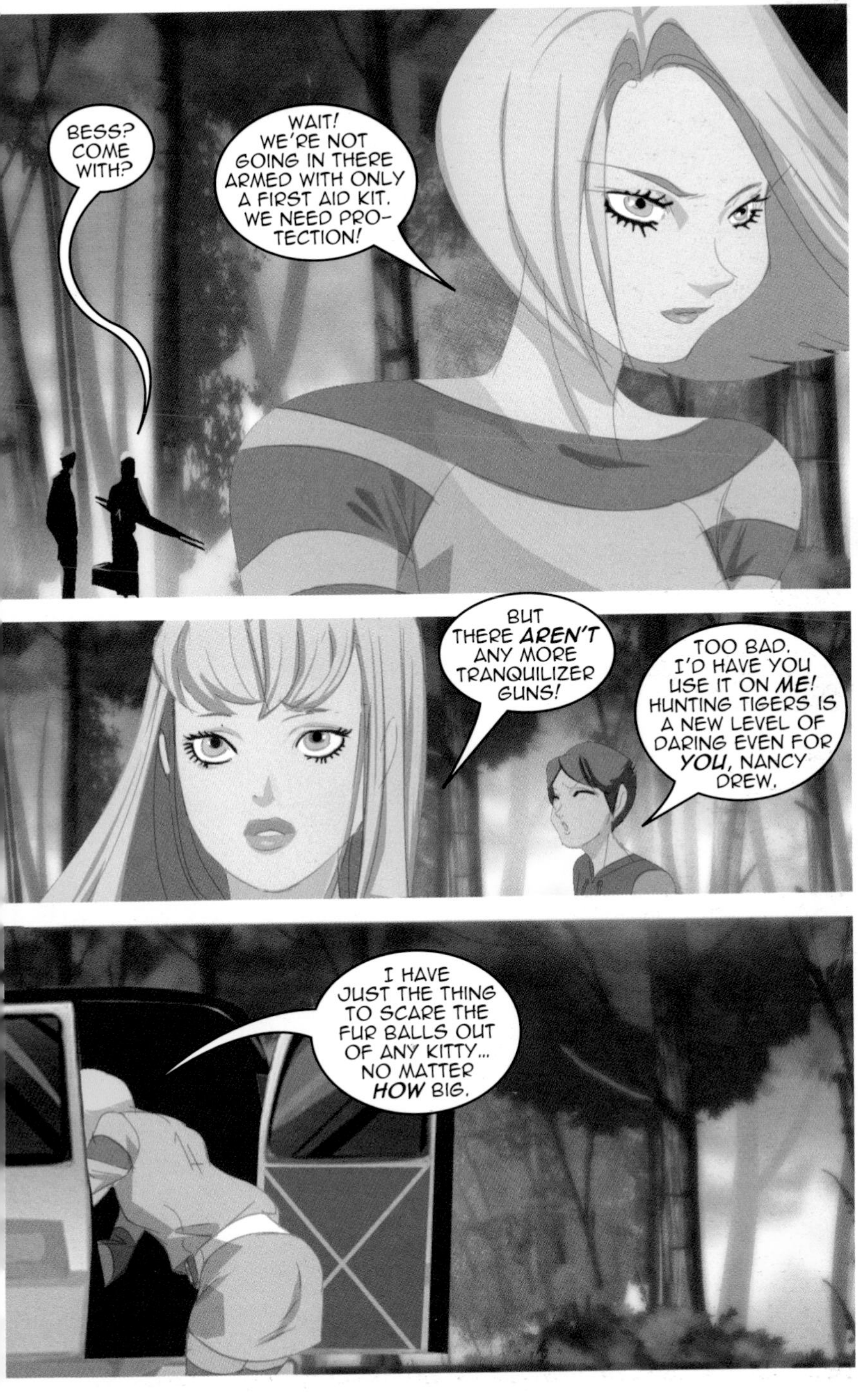
BESS? COME WITH?
WAIT! WE'RE NOT GOING IN THERE ARMED WITH ONLY A FIRST AID KIT. WE NEED PRO-TECTION!
BUT THERE AREN'T ANY MORE TRANQUILIZER GUNS!
TOO BAD. I'D HAVE YOU USE IT ON ME! HUNTING TIGERS IS A NEW LEVEL OF DARING EVEN FOR YOU, NANCY DREW.
I HAVE JUST THE THING TO SCARE THE FUR BALLS OUT OF ANY KITTY... NO MATTER HOW BIG.

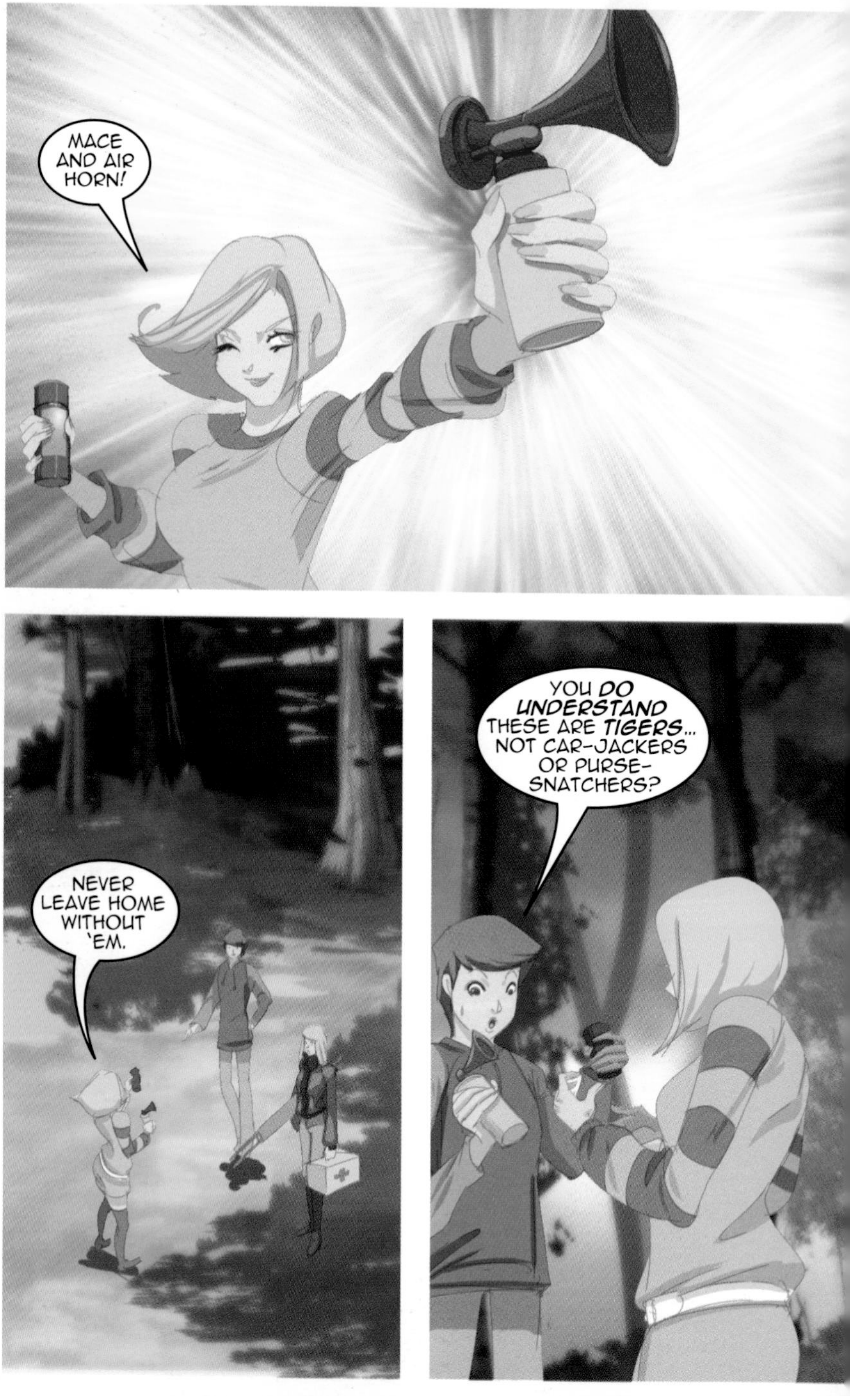
MACE AND AIR HORN!
NEVER LEAVE HOME WITHOUT 'EM.
YOU DO UNDERSTAND THESE ARE TIGERS... NOT CAR-JACKERS OR PURSE-SNATCHERS?

SPEAKING OF JACK, YOU KNOW, I THINK HE MADE AN EXCELLENT POINT ABOUT LOSING LIMBS AND STAYING IN THE CAR.

THEY CALL THEM *MAN*-EATING TIGERS, BUT I FIGURE THEY'RE JUST AS LIKELY TO BE *GIRL*-EATING!

NOT HELP-FUL.

NOT SO MUCH.

LOOK! MORE TRACKS OVER THERE!

WHA?

LOOK! OVER *HERE*, TOO! THERE ARE TRACKS ALL OVER THE PLACE!

HEY!

MY PALS HAVE BOLDLY FACED CRIMINALS OF ALL SHAPES AND EVILNESS.

SO I WAS SURPRISED TO SEE THEM SO *JITTERY* ABOUT ANIMALS WHO, AS FAR AS WE KNEW, HAD COMMITTED NO CRIME AT ALL!

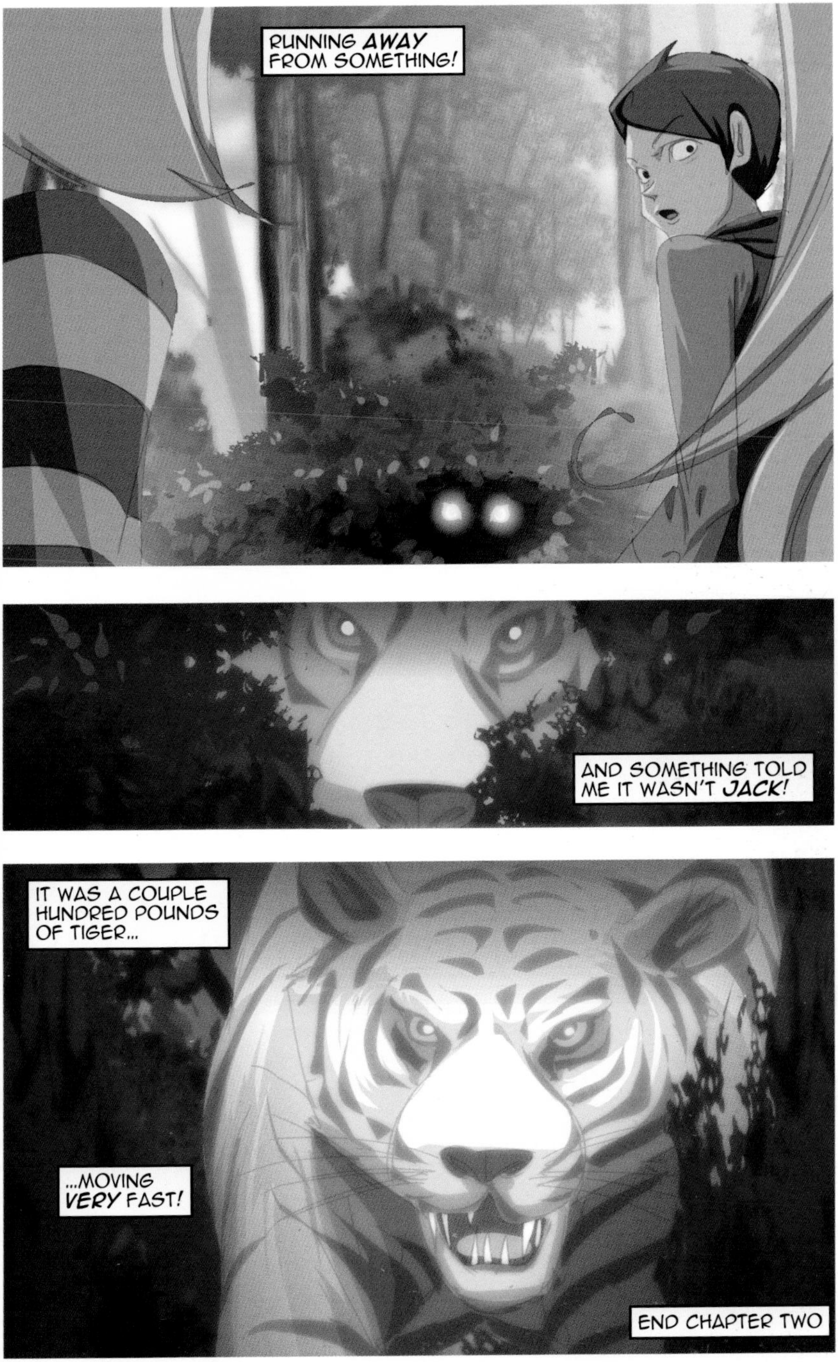
RUNNING *AWAY* FROM SOMETHING!
AND SOMETHING TOLD ME IT WASN'T *JACK*!
IT WAS A COUPLE HUNDRED POUNDS OF TIGER...
...MOVING *VERY* FAST!
END CHAPTER TWO

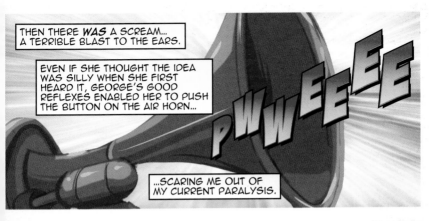

THEN THERE *WAS* A SCREAM... A TERRIBLE BLAST TO THE EARS.

EVEN IF SHE THOUGHT THE IDEA WAS SILLY WHEN SHE FIRST HEARD IT, GEORGE'S GOOD REFLEXES ENABLED HER TO PUSH THE BUTTON ON THE AIR HORN...

...SCARING ME OUT OF MY CURRENT PARALYSIS.

THE PAINFUL BLAST *DISTRACTED* THE TIGER...

...FOR A SECOND.

BUT, RATHER THAN SCARING IT *AWAY*...

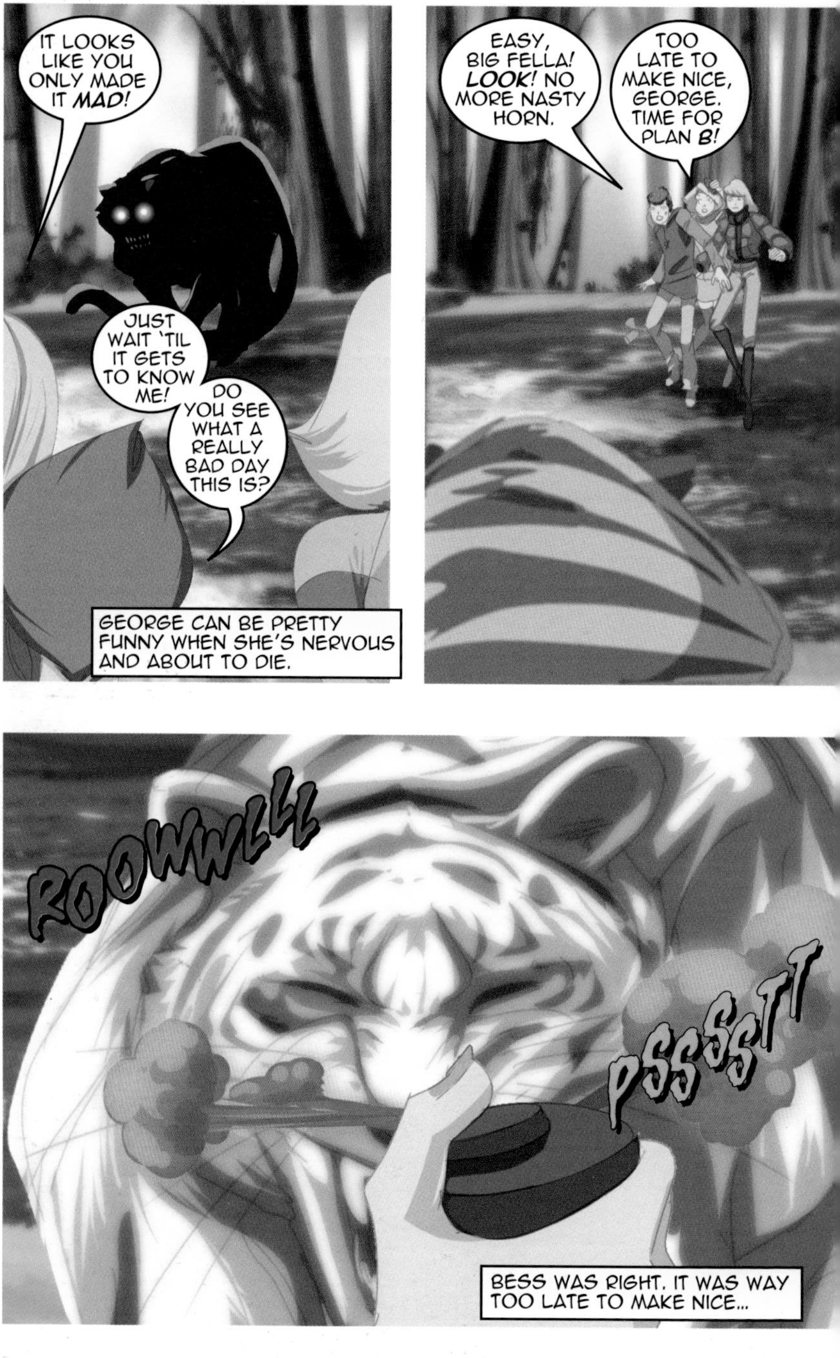

IT LOOKS LIKE YOU ONLY MADE IT *MAD*!
JUST WAIT 'TIL IT GETS TO KNOW ME!
DO YOU SEE WHAT A REALLY BAD DAY THIS IS?
GEORGE CAN BE PRETTY FUNNY WHEN SHE'S NERVOUS AND ABOUT TO DIE.
EASY, BIG FELLA! ***LOOK!*** NO MORE NASTY HORN.
TOO LATE TO MAKE NICE, GEORGE. TIME FOR PLAN ***B***!
ROOWWLLL
PSSSSTT
BESS WAS RIGHT. IT WAS WAY TOO LATE TO MAKE NICE...

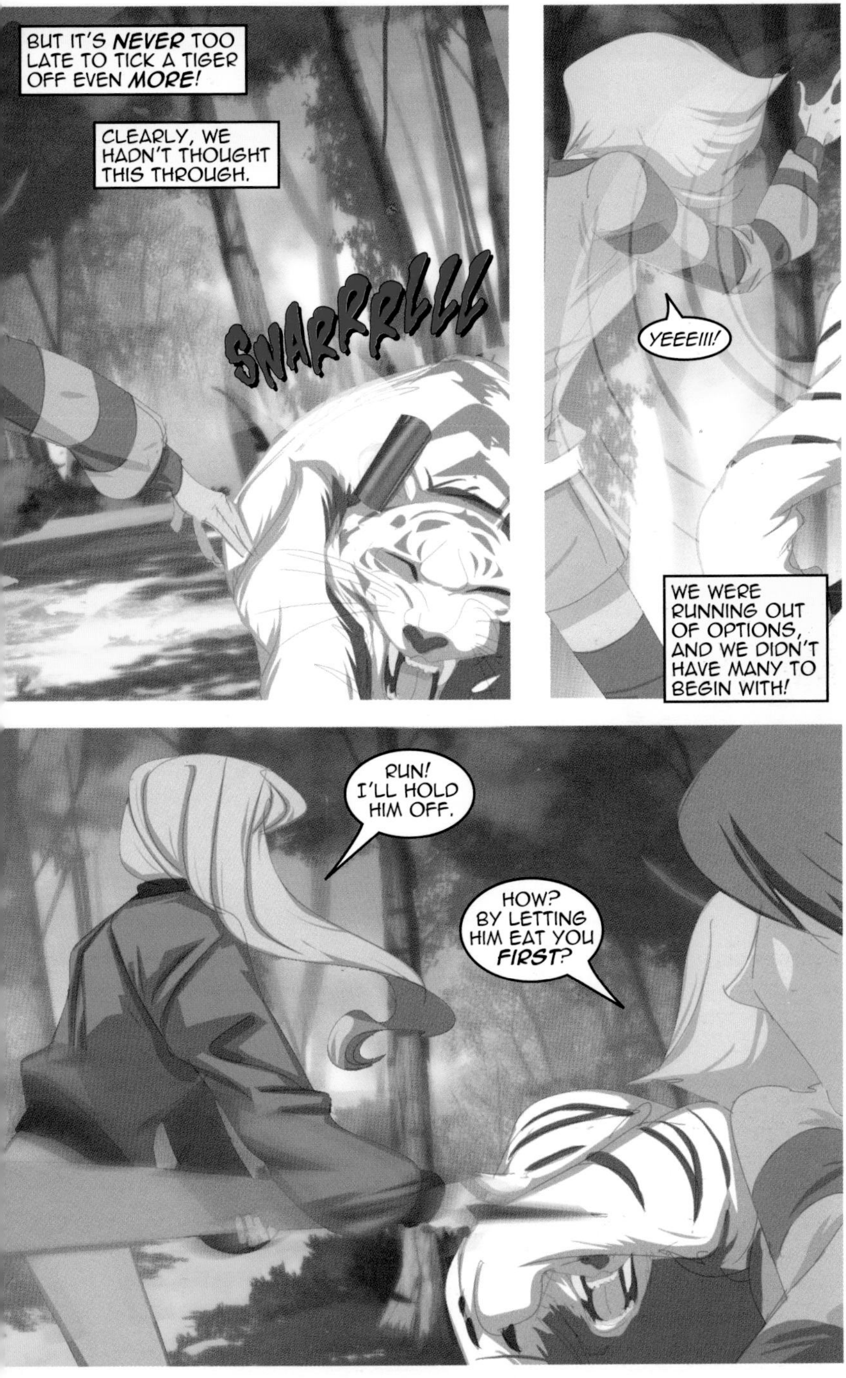
BUT IT'S *NEVER* TOO LATE TO TICK A TIGER OFF EVEN *MORE*!
CLEARLY, WE HADN'T THOUGHT THIS THROUGH.
SNARRRLLL
YEEEIII!
WE WERE RUNNING OUT OF OPTIONS, AND WE DIDN'T HAVE MANY TO BEGIN WITH!
RUN! I'LL HOLD HIM OFF.
HOW? BY LETTING HIM EAT YOU *FIRST*?

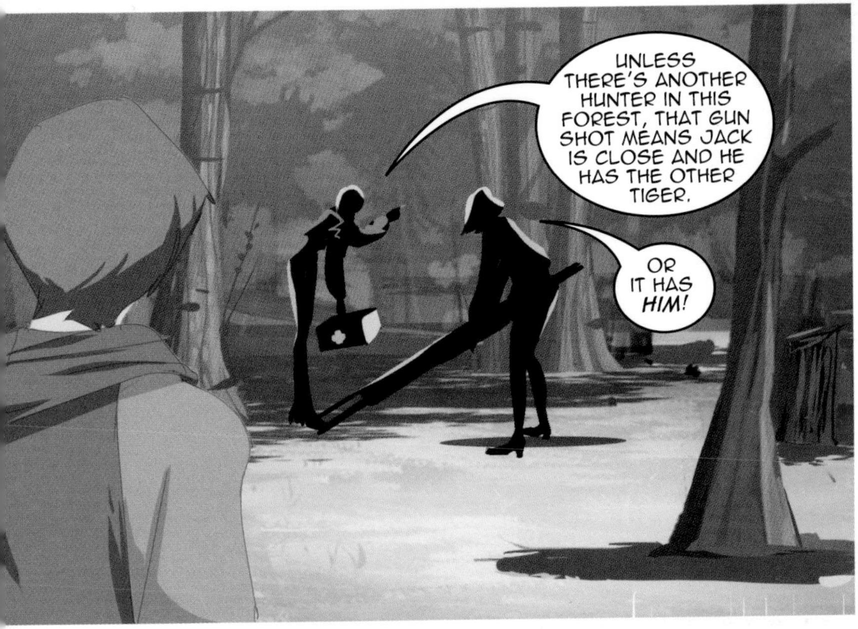
UNLESS THERE'S ANOTHER HUNTER IN THIS FOREST, THAT GUN SHOT MEANS JACK IS CLOSE AND HE HAS THE OTHER TIGER.
OR IT HAS *HIM!*

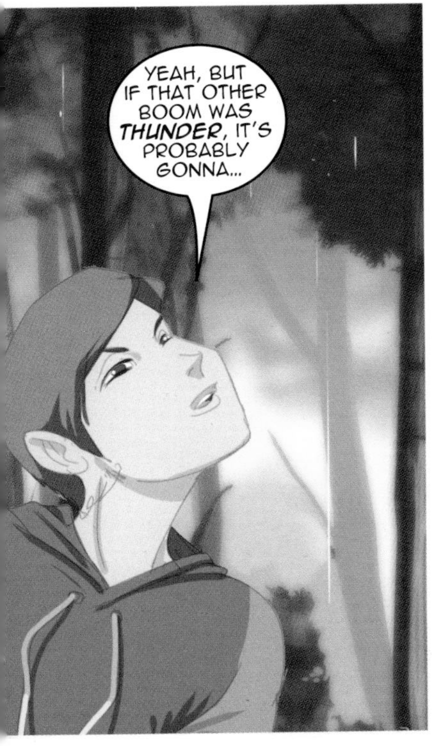
YEAH, BUT IF THAT OTHER BOOM WAS *THUNDER*, IT'S PROBABLY GONNA...

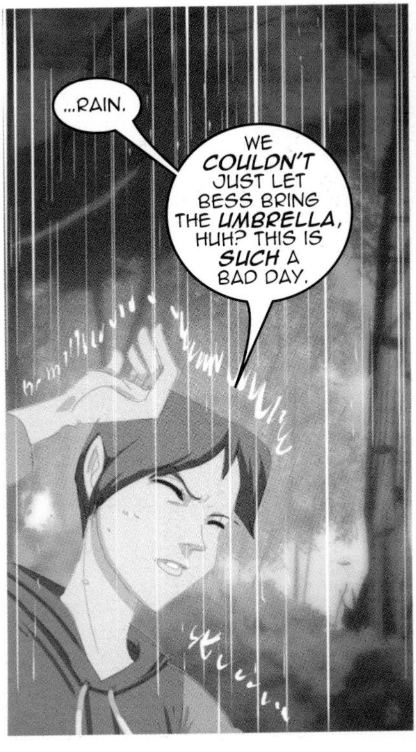
...RAIN.
WE *COULDN'T* JUST LET BESS BRING THE *UMBRELLA*, HUH? THIS IS *SUCH* A BAD DAY.

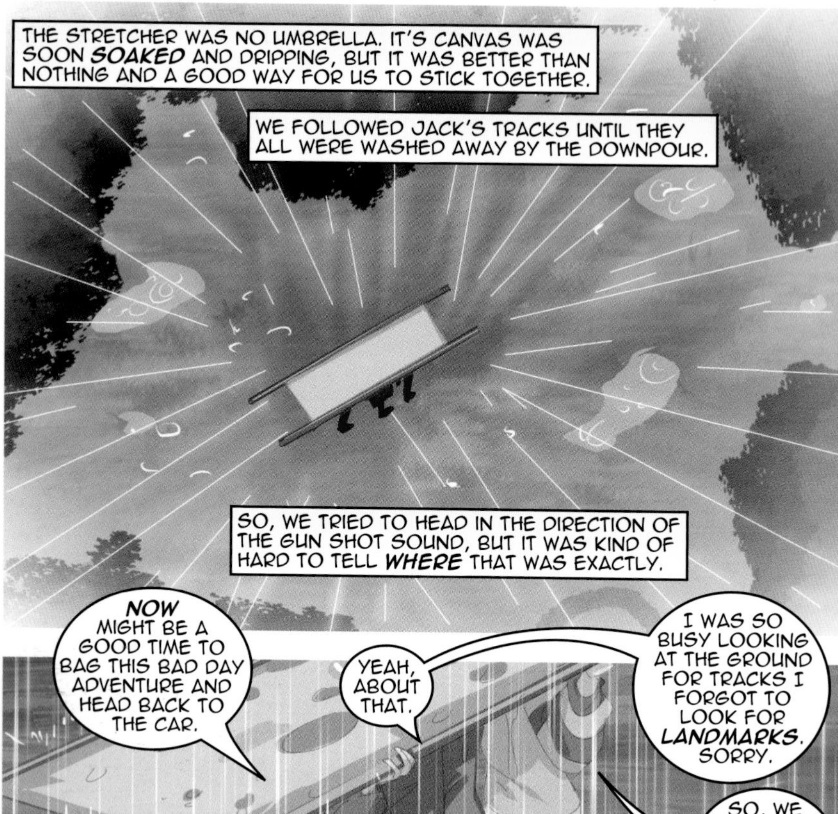
THE STRETCHER WAS NO UMBRELLA. IT'S CANVAS WAS SOON *SOAKED* AND DRIPPING, BUT IT WAS BETTER THAN NOTHING AND A GOOD WAY FOR US TO STICK TOGETHER.
WE FOLLOWED JACK'S TRACKS UNTIL THEY ALL WERE WASHED AWAY BY THE DOWNPOUR.
SO, WE TRIED TO HEAD IN THE DIRECTION OF THE GUN SHOT SOUND, BUT IT WAS KIND OF HARD TO TELL *WHERE* THAT WAS EXACTLY.
NOW MIGHT BE A GOOD TIME TO BAG THIS BAD DAY ADVENTURE AND HEAD BACK TO THE CAR.
YEAH, ABOUT THAT.
I WAS SO BUSY LOOKING AT THE GROUND FOR TRACKS I FORGOT TO LOOK FOR *LANDMARKS*. SORRY.
SO, WE HAVE *NO IDEA* WHERE WE'RE GOING?
BASICALLY.
WE'LL STICK TO HIGH GROUND SO THAT WE DON'T GET STUCK IN A FLOODED SWAMP.
WOULDN'T *THAT* BE A FINE END TO THIS PERFECT DAY?

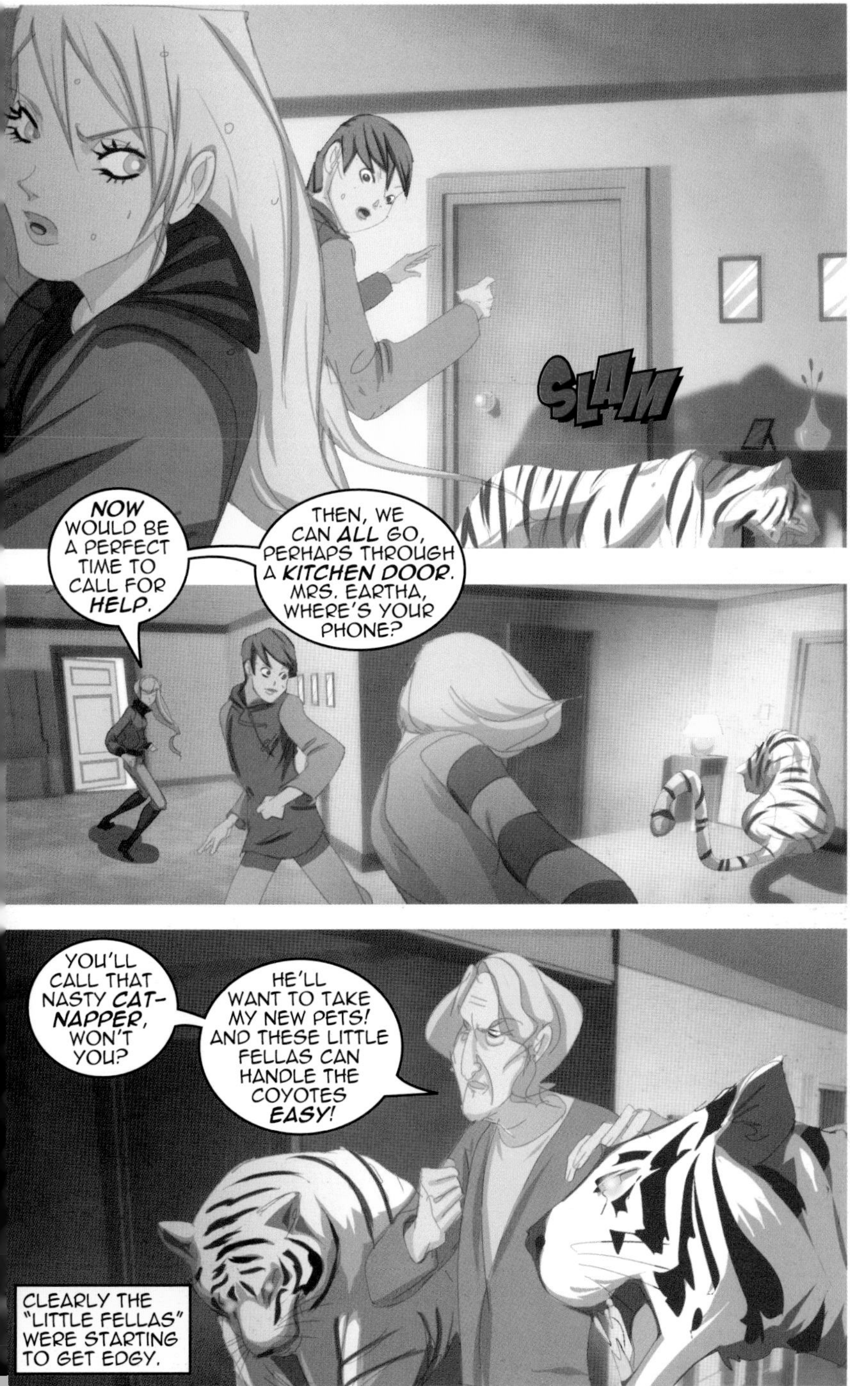
SLAM
NOW WOULD BE A PERFECT TIME TO CALL FOR HELP.
THEN, WE CAN ALL GO, PERHAPS THROUGH A KITCHEN DOOR. MRS. EARTHA, WHERE'S YOUR PHONE?
YOU'LL CALL THAT NASTY CAT-NAPPER, WON'T YOU?
HE'LL WANT TO TAKE MY NEW PETS! AND THESE LITTLE FELLAS CAN HANDLE THE COYOTES EASY!
CLEARLY THE "LITTLE FELLAS" WERE STARTING TO GET EDGY.

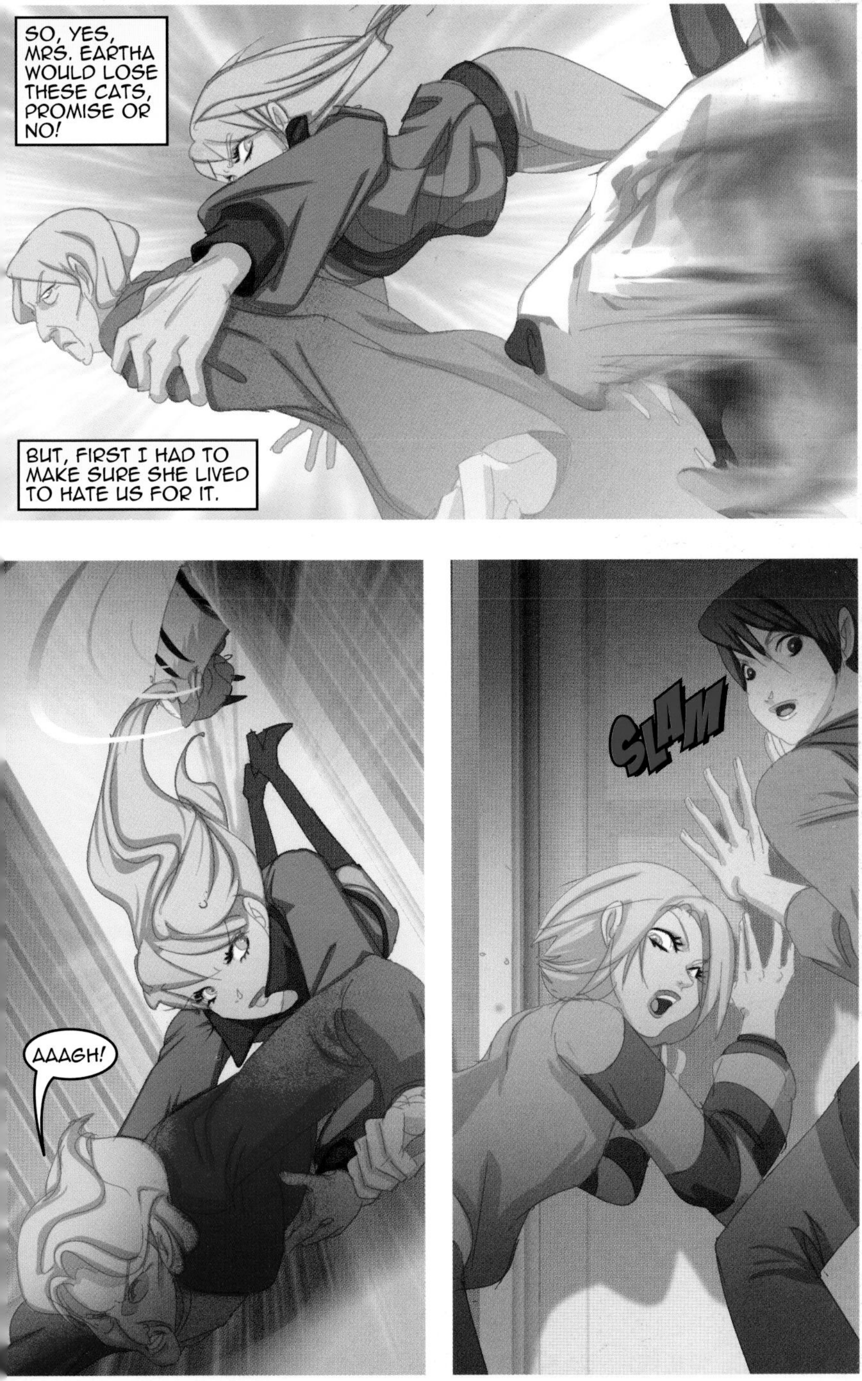
SO, YES, MRS. EARTHA WOULD LOSE THESE CATS, PROMISE OR NO!
BUT, FIRST I HAD TO MAKE SURE SHE LIVED TO HATE US FOR IT.
AAAGH!
SLAM

SORRY, MRS. EARTHA, BUT HUNGRY TIGERS AREN'T GREAT COMPANY.

WE'RE LUCKY THEY'RE CONTAINED IN *THERE*, WHILE WE CALL FOR HELP AND *LEAVE* THROUGH...

...OR NOT.

APPARENTLY THIS HAD BEEN A *HUNTER'S COTTAGE* AND MRS. EARTHA HAD NEVER CHANGED IT TO MATCH THE NEW SAFETY CODES!

NO BACK DOOR! *NO* WINDOW! BEST OF ALL, *NO* PHONE!

OF COURSE NOT! PHONE'S BY MY BED. YOU CAN'T TALK WHILE YOU *EAT*, FOR HEAVEN'S SAKE.

WE'RE TRAPPED, LIKE SWAMP DEER!

AHHH!

WHUMP

ROARRR

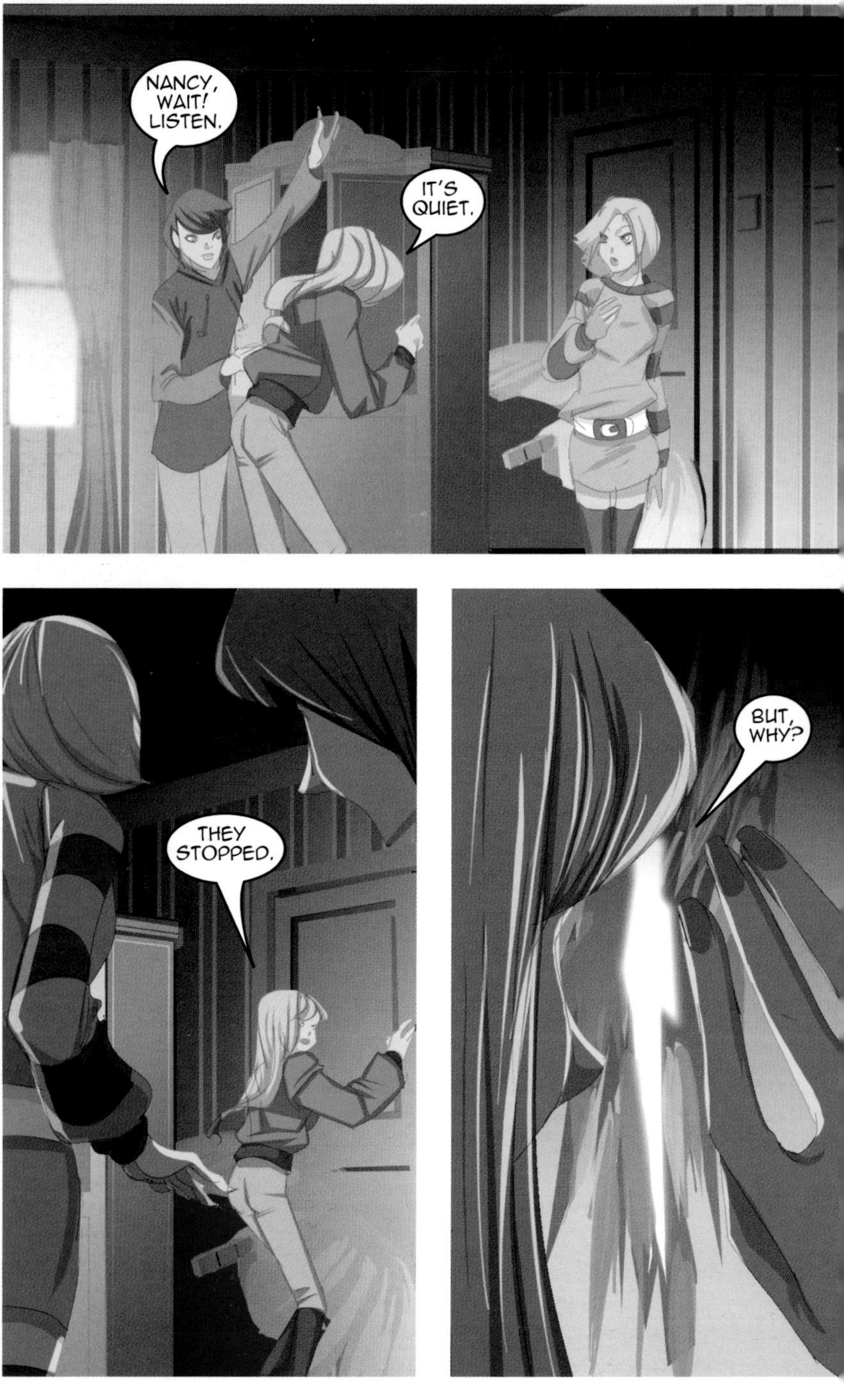
NANCY, WAIT! LISTEN.
IT'S QUIET.
THEY STOPPED.
BUT, WHY?

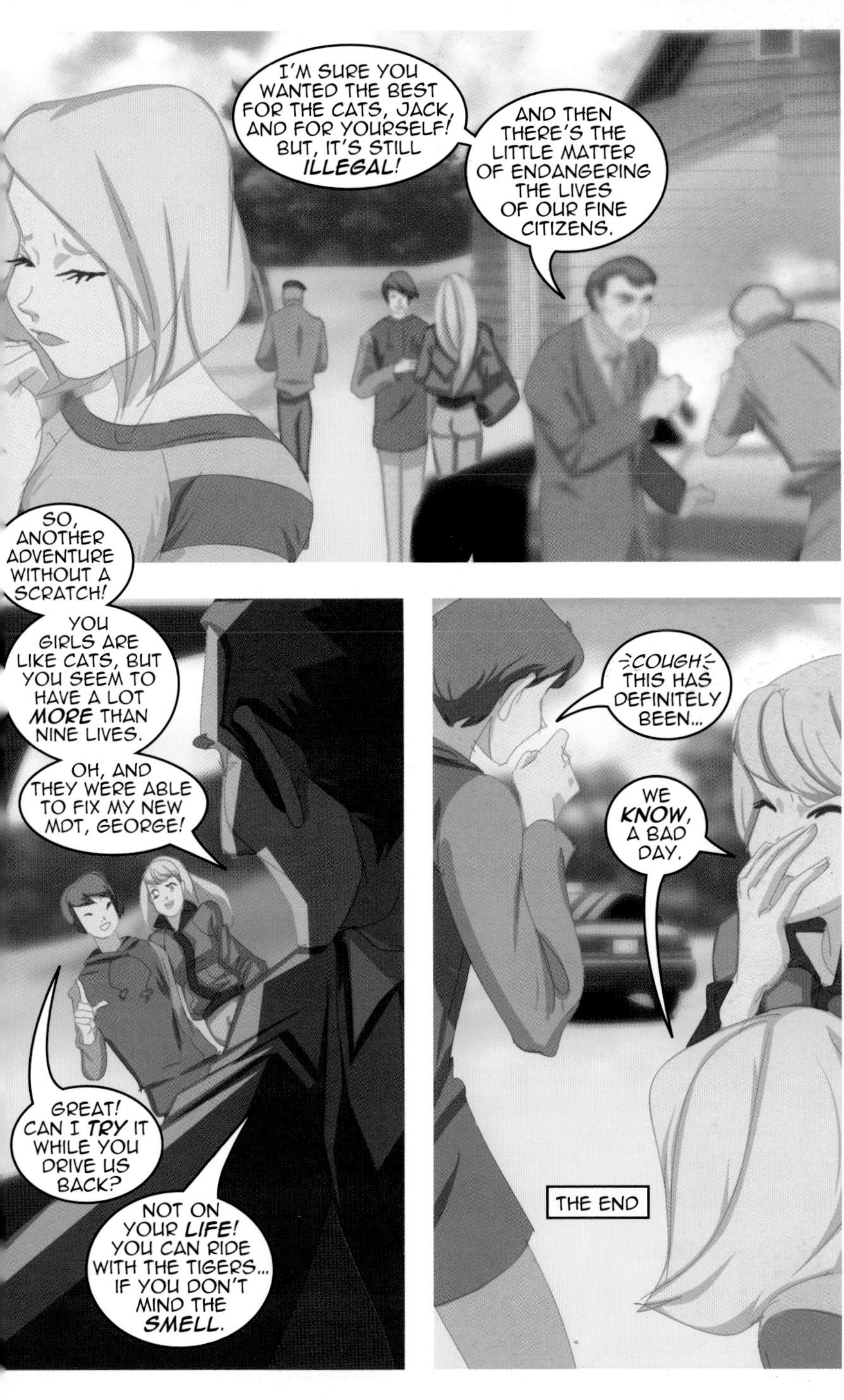
I'M SURE YOU WANTED THE BEST FOR THE CATS, JACK, AND FOR YOURSELF! BUT, IT'S STILL ILLEGAL!
AND THEN THERE'S THE LITTLE MATTER OF ENDANGERING THE LIVES OF OUR FINE CITIZENS.
SO, ANOTHER ADVENTURE WITHOUT A SCRATCH!
YOU GIRLS ARE LIKE CATS, BUT YOU SEEM TO HAVE A LOT MORE THAN NINE LIVES.
OH, AND THEY WERE ABLE TO FIX MY NEW MDT, GEORGE!
GREAT! CAN I TRY IT WHILE YOU DRIVE US BACK?
NOT ON YOUR LIFE! YOU CAN RIDE WITH THE TIGERS... IF YOU DON'T MIND THE SMELL.
COUGH THIS HAS DEFINITELY BEEN...
WE KNOW, A BAD DAY.
THE END

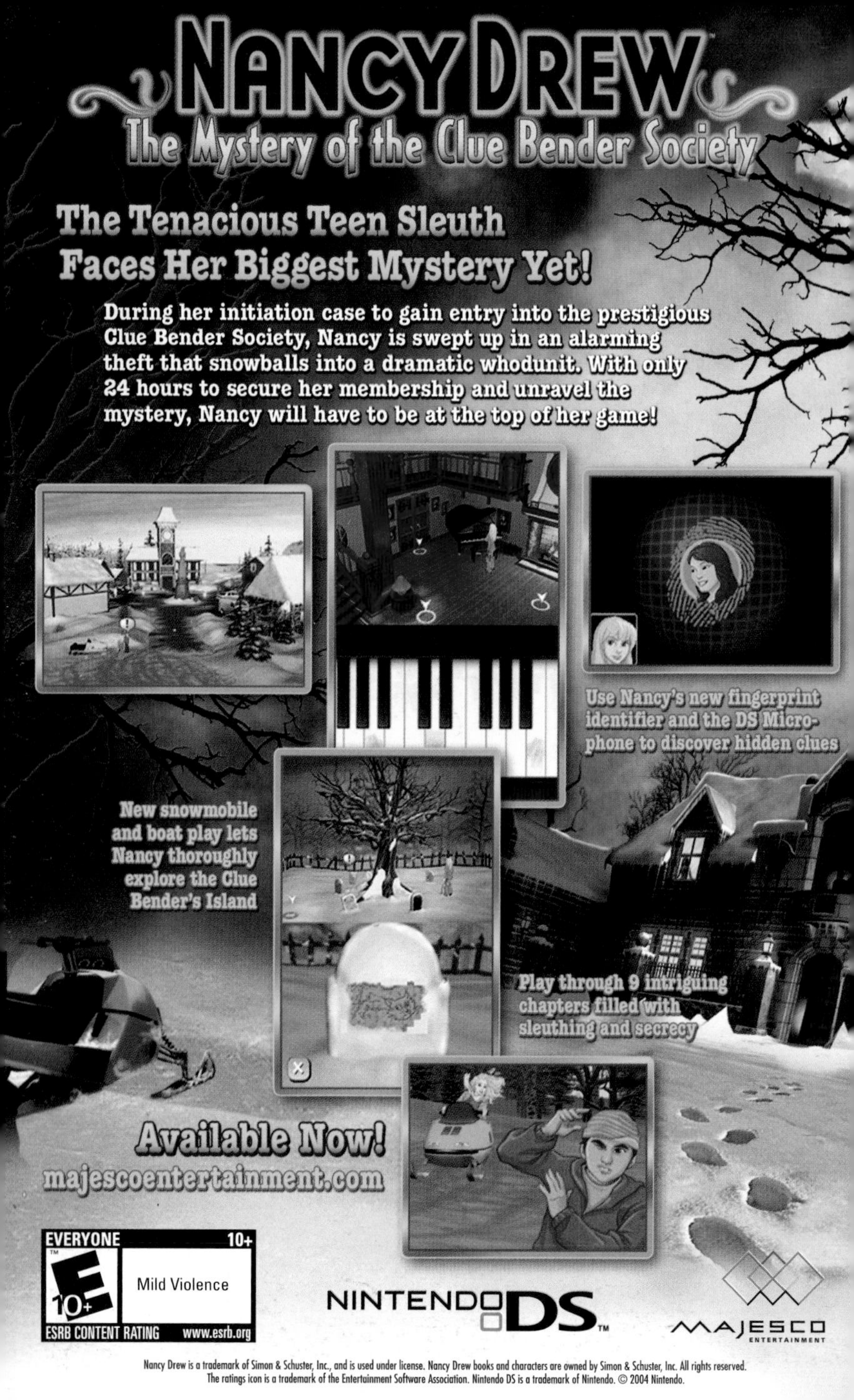
NANCY DREW
The Mystery of the Clue Bender Society
The Tenacious Teen Sleuth Faces Her Biggest Mystery Yet!
During her initiation case to gain entry into the prestigious Clue Bender Society, Nancy is swept up in an alarming theft that snowballs into a dramatic whodunit. With only 24 hours to secure her membership and unravel the mystery, Nancy will have to be at the top of her game!
Use Nancy's new fingerprint identifier and the DS Microphone to discover hidden clues
New snowmobile and boat play lets Nancy thoroughly explore the Clue Bender's Island
Play through 9 intriguing chapters filled with sleuthing and secrecy
Available Now!
majescoentertainment.com
EVERYONE 10+
E 10+
Mild Violence
ESRB CONTENT RATING www.esrb.org
NINTENDO DS
MAJESCO ENTERTAINMENT
Nancy Drew is a trademark of Simon & Schuster, Inc., and is used under license. Nancy Drew books and characters are owned by Simon & Schuster, Inc. All rights reserved.
The ratings icon is a trademark of the Entertainment Software Association. Nintendo DS is a trademark of Nintendo. © 2004 Nintendo.

SPECIAL PREVIEW OF NANCY DREW GRAPHIC NOVEL #16 – "WHAT GOES UP..."

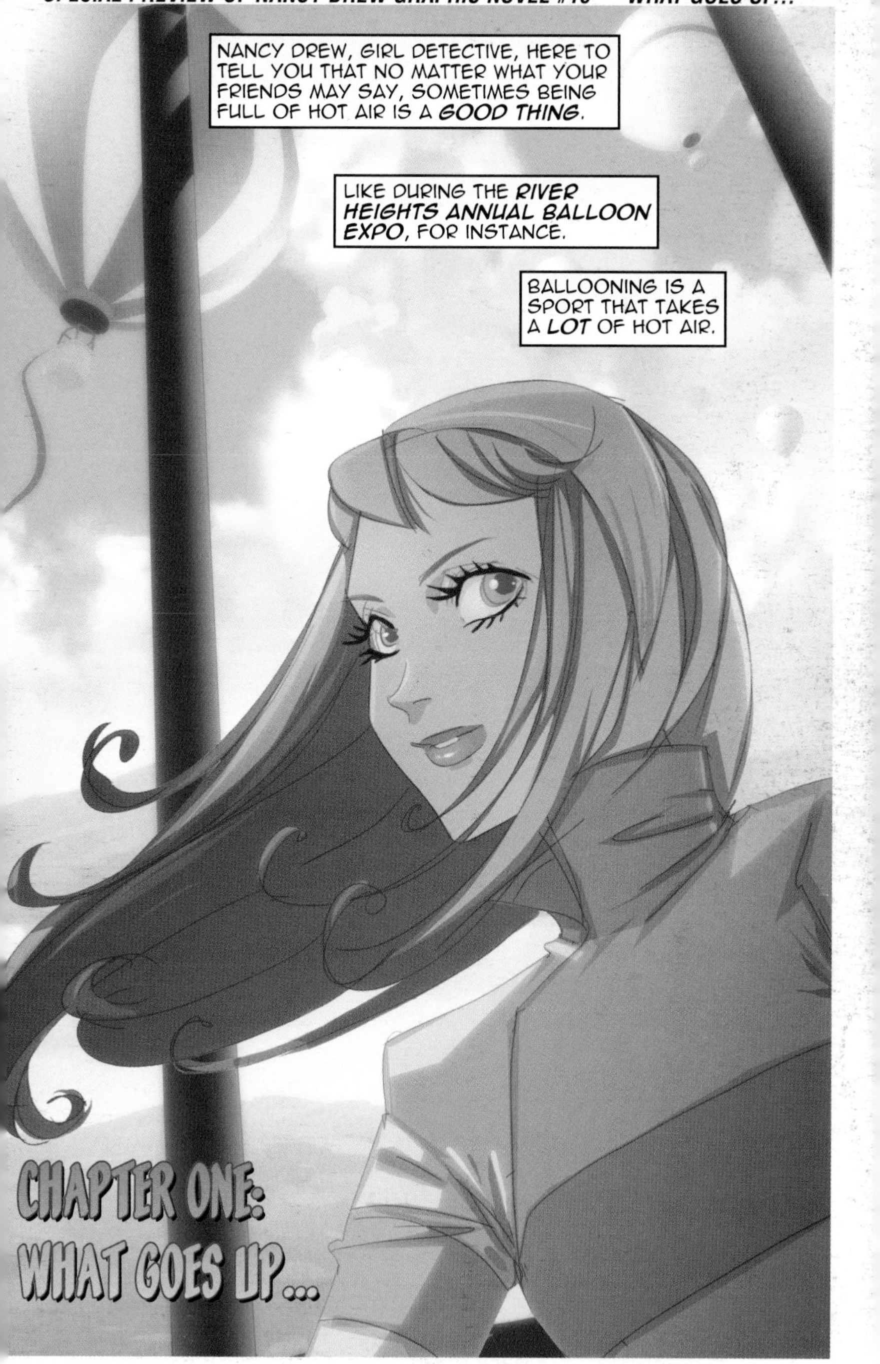
NANCY DREW, GIRL DETECTIVE, HERE TO TELL YOU THAT NO MATTER WHAT YOUR FRIENDS MAY SAY, SOMETIMES BEING FULL OF HOT AIR IS A *GOOD THING*.
LIKE DURING THE *RIVER HEIGHTS ANNUAL BALLOON EXPO*, FOR INSTANCE.
BALLOONING IS A SPORT THAT TAKES A *LOT* OF HOT AIR.
CHAPTER ONE: WHAT GOES UP...

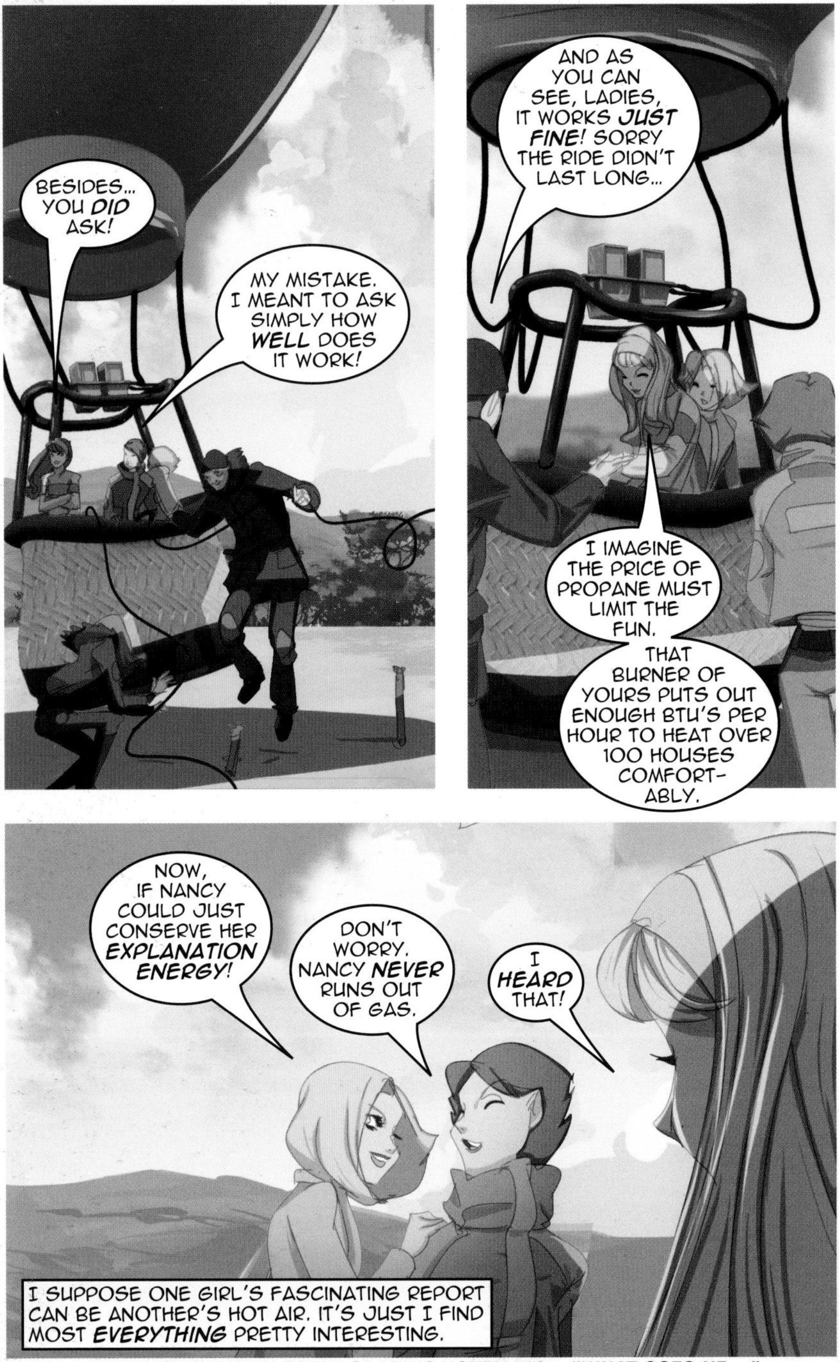
BESIDES... YOU DID ASK!
MY MISTAKE. I MEANT TO ASK SIMPLY HOW WELL DOES IT WORK!
AND AS YOU CAN SEE, LADIES, IT WORKS JUST FINE! SORRY THE RIDE DIDN'T LAST LONG...
I IMAGINE THE PRICE OF PROPANE MUST LIMIT THE FUN.
THAT BURNER OF YOURS PUTS OUT ENOUGH BTU'S PER HOUR TO HEAT OVER 100 HOUSES COMFORT-ABLY.
NOW, IF NANCY COULD JUST CONSERVE HER EXPLANATION ENERGY!
DON'T WORRY. NANCY NEVER RUNS OUT OF GAS.
I HEARD THAT!
I SUPPOSE ONE GIRL'S FASCINATING REPORT CAN BE ANOTHER'S HOT AIR. IT'S JUST I FIND MOST EVERYTHING PRETTY INTERESTING.

DON'T MISS NANCY DREW GRAPHIC NOVEL #16 – "WHAT GOES UP..."

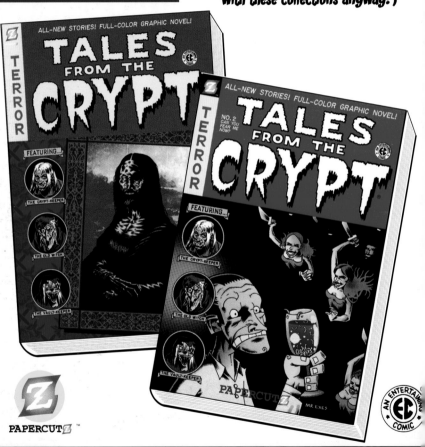

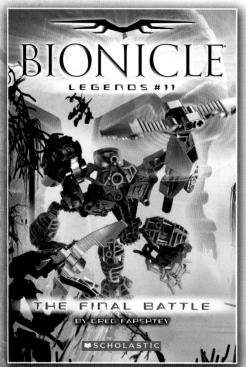

WATCH OUT FOR PAPERCUTZ

Guess what? If you're reading this, that means you may be a Papercutz person. Don't panic -- that's a good thing. It means you're not only enjoying the latest, greatest Nancy Drew graphic novel, but you're part of a special club that's on the cutting edge of pop culture entertainment.

Let's back up a little. If you're just joining the Papercutz party, allow me to indroduce myself. I'm Jim Salicrup, Papercutz Editor-in-Chief. It's my happy responsibility to produce the best graphic novels for people of all ages. Graphic novels, as I'm sure you're hip enough to know, are simply comicbooks disguised as regular books. Or as some people say "real books."

Graphic novels also happen to be the latest thing to take the publishing world by storm. Just a few years ago, only comic-book publishers produced graphic novels, but now just about every big-time publisher there is wants to get in on the act. And you know, we think that's terrific. The more publishers giving opportunities to writers and artists to create all-new graphic novels, the greater the chances are that we'll get to see some amazing new graphic novels from new writers and artists.

On the other hand, with so many graphic novels being produced at such a rapid rate -- more now than ever before -- it's easy to be completely overwhelmed by it all. How can anyone know which graphic novels to choose, with so many to pick from? Well, we have one helpful suggestion. If you like the graphic novel you're reading now, chances are you may enjoy other Papercutz graphic novels. In the following pages, you'll find some sample pages from TALES FROM THE CRYPT, which features several scary stories within each volume.

So, check us out. If you like what you see, you may just be a Papercutz person. And, as we said, that's a good thing.

Thanks,

THE OLD EDITOR

Caricature by Rick Parker

–Greetings, Fiends!

It's your ol' pal the CRYPT-KEEPER here, giving a guided TERRIFYING TOUR through the SCARIEST GRAPHIC NOVEL ever! It's TALES FROM THE CRYPT #4 "CRYPT-KEEPING IT REAL."

You'll not only find page after page of PULSE-POUNDING CHILLS, but me and my fellow GhouLunatics decided to get all COMPUTER AGE-Y on you! Wait till you see the stories we found on the INTERRED-NET site known as YOU-TOOMB! The SHOCKS and SUSPENSE come at you FAST and FURIOUS!

But that's not all! Just gaze upon the CREEPY COVER on the next page, if you DARE! That poor guy made the UNFORTUNATE MISTAKE of appearing on a REALITY TV SHOW that was perhaps a little TOO REAL! The show is called "JUMPING THE SHARK" and you can see a quick preview starting right after the next PUTRID PAGE!

THE CRYPT-KEEPER

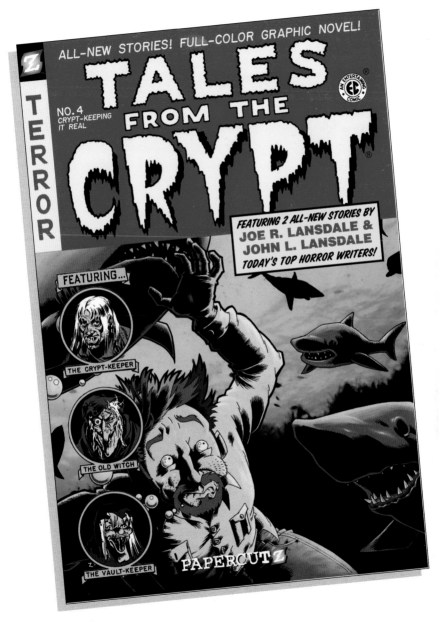

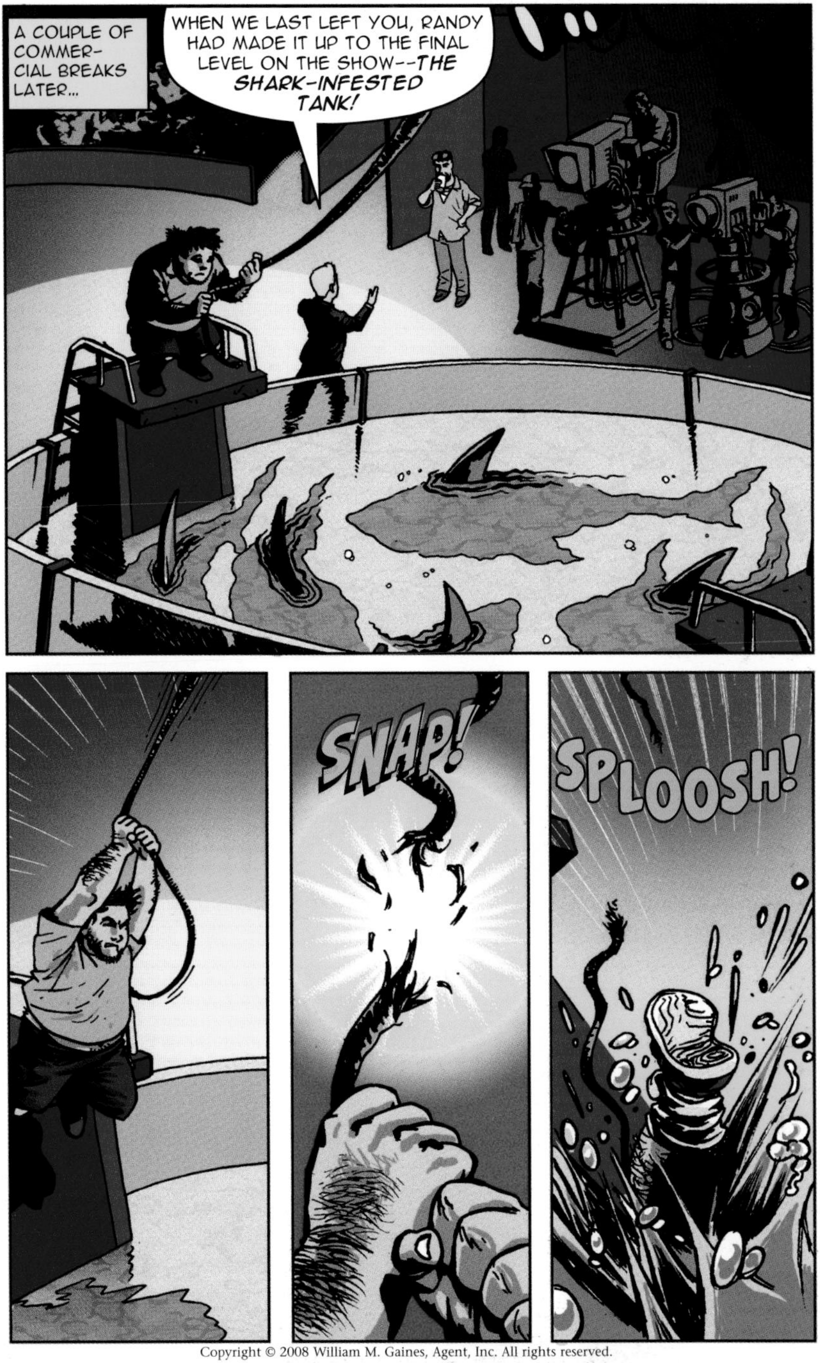
A COUPLE OF COMMER-CIAL BREAKS LATER...
WHEN WE LAST LEFT YOU, RANDY HAD MADE IT UP TO THE FINAL LEVEL ON THE SHOW--*THE SHARK-INFESTED TANK!*
SNAP!
SPLOOSH!